TALES FROM T[...]

Have you ever wondered abou[...] [adver]tisements in your local newspap[...] discount psychotherapy, Gothic[...] seeking to re-establish contact v[...] [...] passed in the night?

    Each book in the *Tales from the Back Page* series looks closely at an advertisement placed on the "Bulletin Board" of *The Clarion*, a community newspaper published on Manhattan's Upper West Side. In the first volume, *Who Gets the Apartment?*, a con artist dupes four young Manhattanites, renting them a luxury penthouse condo (which he doesn't own) for $600 a month. When the four strangers attempt to move into the apartment on the same day, they realize they've been had. Which of them, if any, will get to keep the apartment? Will they band together to bring the swindler to justice, or will they connive and plot against one another?

    In Volume 2, *Circle of Assassins*, five disgruntled New Yorkers find themselves manipulated into murder by a criminal mastermind. Hailed as a masterpiece of suspense filled with shocking surprises, *Circle of Assassins* explores what happens when average people decide to take justice into their own hands.

    Check your bookstore regularly for future volumes in the *Tales from the Back Page* series.

Available Now:
#1. Who Gets the Apartment? / Good Boys Never Win
#2. Circle of Assassins

Coming Soon:
#3. Androgynous Murder House Party / Faith, Hope, and Charity
#4. Three Women

Circle of Assassins

Tales from the Back Page #2

Steven Rigolosi

Copyright © 2007 by Steven Rigolosi

Requests for permission to make copies of any part of the work should be e-mailed to editorial@ransomnotepress.com.

www.ransomnotepress.com

First U.S. edition

Library of Congress Cataloging-in-Publication Data
Rigolosi, Steven A.
  Circle of assassins / Steven Rigolosi. — 1st U.S. ed.
    p. cm. — (Tales from the back page ; #2)
  Summary: "A dark tale of justice and revenge in which five desperate strangers agree to a murderous plan: Kill someone chosen by a fellow assassin, and in return have a stranger murder a victim of your choice"—Provided by publisher.
  ISBN-13: 978-0-9773787-4-6 (pbk.)
  ISBN-10: 0-9773787-4-8 (pbk.)
  I. Title.
  PS3618.I43C57 2007
  813'.6—dc22
                    2006025986

Published in the United States and Canada by
Ransom Note Press, Ridgewood, NJ

10 9 8 7 6 5 4 3 2 1

Printed in the United States of America

ISBN-13: 978-0-9773787-4-6
ISBN-10: 0-9773787-4-8

For The Partridge

REVENGE IS SWEET!

Every day we are brutalized by those who hurt us, take advantage of us, steal what is ours, mistreat our loved ones, destroy our property, terrorize us psychologically, criticize and condemn us, or trample our self-respect. Enough is enough! It's time to turn the tables. Write to A care of Box 270. (For entertainment purposes only.)

I don't think anyone would disagree that the world is better off without drug dealers, especially when they're living in your neighborhood and the police won't help you....

...because theres no way im letting that guy into my family, i see what happens when people like him are let in, he will ruin everything and someone has to protect my sister....

This seems like a rare opportunity to eliminate someone who merges racism, sexism, and elitism into one disgusting whole. We're doing the world a favor.

...There is no greater betrayal, and no more immoral act, than to misuse the public trust and abuse your power for personal gain. My "chosen" is a low-profile public figure, one who preys on the innocent while pretending to be an upstanding citizen.

Listen, this one's a no-brainer. Nobody thinks child molesters should go on living. The legal system won't get rid of him, so I have to.

Part 1

A

Congratulations. You have made the final cut, partly because you were smart enough to rent a P.O. box for our correspondence. Your chosen is clearly someone with whom we no longer need to coexist.

If you choose to join us, you will be one of our Circle of Five. Phase Two begins upon your receipt of this letter. Your decision will be due in two weeks, at which time I must receive a letter from you with the following detailed information:

- The name and address of your chosen, including apartment number if relevant.
- The phone number of your chosen.
- A recent photo of the chosen.
- The reason(s) you've selected your chosen. The more information you provide, the better. Remember that your colleagues will rely on this information for motivation.
- Any additional information you feel may be helpful or worthwhile, including possible dangers and opportunities.

Use a word processing program: Times New Roman, 12 point, double spaced, one-inch margins all around. *Do not* touch the paper with your bare hands, *do not* touch the envelope, and *do not* use fasteners of any type if your letter exceeds one page. Avoid using your own computer to write the letter. If you use a printer in a public location, *do not* leave a copy of your word processing file behind. *Destroy* your electronic document after you've printed your letter. *Do not* keep a copy of your own letter.

Avoid writing your letter by hand, but if you must, write in block capitals with a cheap blue ballpoint pen on a sheet of looseleaf notebook paper.

I also strongly recommend that you close out your current P.O. box and rent a mailbox through a private company such as MailStop USA, whose rules are much more relaxed than those of U.S. government post offices. All these precautions ensure that a case against you, or me, can never be proved based on this correspondence.

Now that I have made the initial cut based on our earlier, more general, correspondence, I will institute the double-blind system we have discussed. Though I will be a member of the Circle, for both your protection and mine I will no longer read your letters. Nor will I keep track of which colleague receives your letter of instruction.

Here is how the system will work. I have assigned you a letter and a corresponding color (red, blue, black, green, or orange). Proceed as follows:

- Sign all correspondence with the alphabet letter you've been assigned.
- Place your letter in a plain white envelope. *Again, do not touch the envelope with your bare hands.* On the back of the envelope, write two of the colors *not* assigned to you (see list above).
- Place your envelope inside another envelope and send it to the specified post office box. You will receive information about this P.O. box under separate cover. Each member of our circle has been assigned a separate P.O. box.

Further instructions will follow.

If I do not receive your letter of instruction within two weeks, I will assume that you have removed yourself from the Circle.

 A.

B

Black, Orange

To Whom It May Concern:

Though I will never meet you, I want to thank you for your help.

I will provide the necessary information below, but first I would like you to understand why I have been driven to these extreme measures.

Have you ever worked hard, so impossibly hard, for something? Have you saved your money for decades, going without vacations, cars, and even meals so that you could purchase something that would last you a lifetime? And then, after you've worked and slaved, someone comes along to ruin everything?

That is exactly what has happened to me, and I'm not going to put up with it any longer. I have worked too hard for too long, and I'm not going to sit by idly while one man destroys my life.

Please understand, I am not a cruel, malicious, or evil person. But I have decided to stand up for myself. To fight for what I worked so hard for.

For the first six decades of my life, I lived in a tenement building in the Bronx. In the old days, that part of the Bronx wasn't so bad. All the apartments were filled with immigrants whose youngest children were the first to be born in America. None of us had a lot of money (nobody did in the years after the Depression), but the building was always clean and safe. But over the decades, the neighborhood changed little by little. One day I woke up and I realized: *I live in the ghetto*. For the last two years before I left, I used to literally nail my apartment door shut each night. Everyone else who lived on my floor had been mugged or robbed in the previous twelve months, and I couldn't let that happen to me. Because my way out was hidden in the apartment, and I was terrified that someone would take it from me.

My father had died when I was quite young, and for a few years my mother made ends meet by working on the assembly line at a factory in Morris Park and doing part-time work as a maid. But she'd never been healthy, and when the factory increased her hours, she kept collapsing on the job. Her maid work lasted until I finished high school, but then her arthritis kicked in. She was bedridden within a year.

There were fewer choices back then. I had to go to work, and I started cleaning houses, too. Just after high school, I'd taken some shorthand classes, so I was able to find a decent full-time job as a secretary with an insurance company. The job paid enough for me and Mother to survive on. We didn't live high, but we got by.

I got small raises every year, usually just enough to cover the rent increases. Maybe you can imagine my frustration at seeing the price of the apartment increasing as the neighborhood got worse. But there was nowhere else to go, and Mother's health was always declining.

I was fortunate that Mother was so kind. She appreciated everything I did for her and lamented that I should be getting married, that my life shouldn't revolve around her. But the truth is, it did. In the big scheme of things, I really didn't mind. I'd dated a little in high school, but I never met anyone I wanted to spend the rest of my life with. Maybe I would have met that someone special if I'd tried harder or gone out more, but I didn't, and it's too late now. My only regret is that I never had any children. I'm basically alone in the world; my only living relative is my cousin Nicholas, who calls me his "aunt" because he's so much younger than I am. He's a wonderful boy, but he's busy doing all the things that thirty-year-olds do, so I don't see much of him, even though we don't live that far apart.

One thing Mother and I used to fantasize about was *space*, a feeling you may not understand if you didn't grow up in an apartment. We'd watch TV and see how the beautiful people lived, with their mansions on rolling acres of gardens and wilderness. We longed to sit in our own backyard, to cut fresh flowers from our garden, to drive a car we couldn't afford into a garage we'd never have. Instead, we had four grimy walls on the fifth floor of a walk-up building, with a view of the Broadway el on one side and a decrepit playground on the other.

I know precisely when the idea started to form...it was the evening of Mother's 60th birthday. She innocently said something like, "Some day, I'm going to die in this apartment. It's both comforting and depressing." And I started crying so hard that I couldn't catch my breath. Of course the thought of Mother dying upset me terribly. But I was also crying tears of self-pity, too, because I knew the same fate awaited me. That night I vowed I was not going to die in that apartment, too.

So I started saving my pennies. It's amazing how cheaply you can live if you're willing to deprive yourself of everyday things that are nice to have but not necessary for survival. Mother still got everything she needed, of course, but I did without. After only a short while, it didn't feel like sacrifice. Staying home and watching TV all night costs no money, except for the electricity, and we were always careful to turn off all the lights while we watched the big black box. Reading is cheap when you borrow books from the library, and it costs nothing to sit, talk, and play cards with your neighbors.

I should have put my money in the bank, I know. But Father had lost everything in banks during the Depression, and my family had never trusted them since. So all my pennies, nickels, and dimes (and even that rare dollar bill) were hidden in the apartment. I was so terrified we'd be robbed that I had more than forty different hiding spots. I didn't keep a list of them because I was afraid someone would find it. I didn't need to, though. I could have recited each and every hidden location in my sleep.

Every once in a while, I'd get a sudden windfall, like a small bonus at work, and it would all go into my sock, or my doll, or my hollowed-out book, or the cookie jar, or the ice box, or behind my picture frame, or underneath my shabby area rug. And over the years, as my hair turned gray, my stash grew.

I did my one selfish thing when Mother died. I had the money to spend on a decent casket for her, but I didn't. I couldn't spend part of my life savings on a box that would be buried in the ground, never to be seen again. So I had Mother cremated, telling myself she would have wanted it that way.

Things did get a little easier in the years following Mother's passing. I missed her terribly, but life went on much as it had before. I kept saving and thought that in another five years or so I'd have the money I needed.

And then a miracle happened. Three months after Mother died, I was struck by a taxi cab while crossing West 230th Street, and my right leg was broken. It was the greatest thing that ever happened to me. The leg healed quickly (it was strong after all those years of climbing up and down the stairs to the apartment), but the man who'd hit me had been driving drunk. I got more money in the settlement than I'd ever seen in my life.

As soon as I could walk again, I started calling real estate agents. For years I'd been researching towns and neighborhoods, and I knew what I wanted. After sixty years in New York City, what I wanted more than anything was *space, solitude,* and *quiet.* Because you can't have any of these things in the Bronx, or anywhere else in the City, I focused my search on the suburbs. Despite the money from the settlement, I certainly wasn't wealthy enough to quit the secretarial job I'd held for forty years, so I needed a place that would allow me to commute into the City fairly easily. Fortunately, as I'd discovered, many towns in New Jersey, New York State, and Long Island have decent train and bus access to Manhattan.

In the third month of my quest, I found it: the sweetest little Cape Cod a person could ever hope for. It was summertime, and the yard was full of hollyhocks and sunflowers. Every one of the four bedrooms had at least two windows. There was a picture window in the kitchen, and even a window in the bathroom! The basement was pristine; so was the attic. I could walk to the bus stop and be at work in a little more than an hour.

I moved in three months to the day after seeing the house for the first time. The down payment took almost all my savings, and buying curtains, carpeting, and used furniture took the rest.

The next few years were a dream. Through watching home improvement shows for so long and borrowing every home improvement book available at the Bloomfield, New Jersey public library, I learned how to make a house look pretty and new on a budget. Nothing like a fresh coat of paint with some faux finishes, which I learned how to do at a free class at the Y, to spruce a place up. Living in an apartment for so long, you learn how not to accumulate junk, so my basement, from the beginning, was clean and uncluttered. To have your own washing machine and your own dryer in your own basement! That alone was worth the price of the house.

My street, my neighborhood, and my town were everything I'd hoped for. The neighbors are friendly and watch out for one another, but we also keep a certain respectful distance. We have a mix of older, established families and younger people who are just starting out. In the summer, lawns are mowed promptly every Saturday morning, and in the winter, snow gets shoveled as it falls. Best of all, my house (yes, my house!) is on a dead-end street, so there's very little traffic and noise. The people who live here are good, honest, hard-working people whose homes are their only asset. So the quality of the neighborhood is important to all of us.

Mother and Father would be so proud to see what I've accomplished. It took me more than 65 years, but for the first time in my life, I have a little extra money to play with. I hadn't expected the tax advantages of owning a house, and now I get a nice tax refund from the IRS every year. With the refund money, I sometimes treat myself to new clothes and shoes, or to a piece of furniture I've had my eye on. Occasionally I go out to Queens to visit my nephew, and I like bringing him small gifts and treating him to the early bird special somewhere. It isn't much, I know, but I wasn't able to help him (financially) after his parents died, and I suppose I'm trying to make up for lost time.

I've gotten used to the peace and tranquillity of my wonderful, modest home. I expected that the joy would go on forever, until I was lying stone cold in the ground alongside Mother. I was wrong. It all changed six months ago when *he* moved into the neighborhood.

His elderly mother had been living on the block for more than fifty years when she died. None of us even knew she had a son—we'd never seen him before. A week after she passed away, a U-Haul pulled up and we watched as a slovenly, straggly-haired man of about forty took out a key and unlocked the front door of Nora's house.

The next night, trucks, motorcycles, and vans from three states descended on our quiet block and plunged us into misery. Profanity-filled music blasted from outdoor loudspeakers until the wee hours. We shut our windows and turned up the air conditioning, thinking it would all be over the next day. But it was just the beginning.

We know he sells drugs. Cars pull up in the middle of the night and leave a few minutes later. Four of the houses on the block have been robbed; two neighbors lost precious heirloom jewelry that had been in the family for generations. One of the drug addicts who buys from this man smashed his car into a tree. The tree toppled onto the home of a sweet elderly gentleman who was nearly killed when it crashed through his bedroom ceiling. The noise never stops, and the police can't, or won't, do anything about it. As soon as they leave, the music starts up again, louder than before.

And the very worst part: The children aren't safe, either. One of his "friends" was driving an SUV too fast and struck a three-year old boy who was playing kickball in front of his house. (The boy lived, thank God.) The pretty teenage girls have been leered at, gawked at, propositioned, threatened. They're afraid to leave their houses without their fathers, brothers, or boyfriends.

A few of us formed a coalition and decided to visit him, to ask him to please show us the respect his mother showed us, and that we showed her in return. He withdrew into the house and returned with a gun, waving it in our faces and threatening to "blow our fucking heads off" if we ever trespassed on his property again. He ended his threats by calling one of my neighbors, a nice man who teaches science in the high school, a "fucking faggot," then pointing at me and telling me to get my smelly old cunt off his front steps. I snapped and slapped his face. He slapped me back. When I cried, "Please, just go somewhere else," he replied, "I'm not going anywhere, lady, so get used to having me around."

Each day brings a new nightmare. We're powerless to do anything. Or I thought we were, until I saw the ad in *The Clarion*, which I like to read at lunchtime.

Here is the information on this animal:

Freddy d'Arget
145 ■■■■ ■■■■■■■ Road
Bloomfield, NJ
973-■■■-1019

He does not work. At least, he doesn't seem to have a job. His house is always busy at nights and on weekends, but I rarely see people visiting on weekdays. He drives a white van that's so dirty it looks gray. It's usually parked backwards on the street in front of his house, yet another indignity to his neighbors. It has California license plates. I have enclosed a picture of him, which appeared in the paper one of the times he was arrested. (He's been arrested several times, but he's always back a couple of days afterwards. I guess the drug business is lucrative enough to pay for good lawyers.)

When you do it, please be careful. Don't forget he has at least one gun in the house. I'm not sure if there are more. There probably are.

I wish you the best of luck. My thoughts, prayers, and thanks are with you.

B

A

It is time to move to Phase Three.

Your assignment is enclosed in a sealed envelope. *Do not* touch the envelope or letter with your hands. Read the letter as many times as necessary to commit to memory the information included within. *Do not* make photocopies or handwritten copies of the letter. As always, these precautions are necessary for your protection, as well as for my safety and that of your colleagues.

Proceed as follows:

Respond to me via the P.O. box number I will send to you under separate cover. In your response, return the assignment letter in its original envelope so that I may ensure that it is destroyed. To indicate that you have accepted the assignment, enclose a subscription card from any magazine.

You will then receive further instructions by mail. *Do not do anything until you receive these instructions.*

You have now committed to this process, and you are expected to fulfill your end of the bargain.

A.

C

red, blue

ok, i'm not good @ writing but heres the info u need.

the guy is roger borelli, 6 ■■■■■■ ■■, throgs neck NY. 718-■■■-9643. cell 917-■■■-1012. he lives in upstairs apt. in 3-family house. if u stand & look @ the house, u will see a door in front & a wooden staircase on the rt. side leading up to a door on the 2nd floor. best way to get into that apt. & get roger is thru that side door @ the top of the staircase.

he works for the phone co. & is gone most of the time. usually out of the apt. by 7 in the a.m. hangs out @ some places in throgs neck & new rochelle, the lido bar & "scamps" & the dew-drop inn. goes to "lacee's" strip club on the throgs neck expwy with his buddies on weekends, or "city lites" night club near the zoo. drives a "transamerica phone" van for work.

roger is about 6 ft tall, maybe 210 or 215. black hair. about 27 yrs old. in the pic, he is the guy in the white shirt on the left side holding a beer. he has goatee in the pic but doesnt have goatee any more.

he is a scumbag, & thats all there is to it.

the asshole thinks he is going to marry my sister, but its not going to happen as long as i have something to say about it.

my family is honorable, we do the right thing. my folks came here from italy when they were teenagers. my father worked his ass off, he saved his money, he sent money home so he could bring his brothers & sisters & mother & father here. then he took care of all of them. he bought supermarkets in the shitass slums of nyc & built them up & stopped the spics from shoplifting & now he is on easy street. & all that time my mother didnt have to work except w/ my father, she got to stay home most of the time & take care of me & my brother & my 2 sisters, which is the way it should be.

my oldest sister married a guy who shows respect & who knows how to behave & who knows how to treat the family. but my baby sister, shes stupid & blind. she sticks up for this asshole (roger) who treats her like shit. he says he loves her & she believes him. but i see (& everyone else does too) how he behaves. he leaves my sister home on fri. & sat. nites so he can hang with his buds @ tittie bars. one of the tittie bars (scamps) has hookers & he goes with them too. he goes to baseball games all summer with his buddies, always leaving my sister alone on weekends so he can have a good time. he is a loser motherfucker cocksucker & he aint marrying my sister, period.

i would do this myself, i want to do it myself. but i cant. everyone would know because i tried a couple of times already. the first time was when i looked up @ a batchelor party for a guy we know & I seen him & his buddies looking up @ the girls dancing on the buffay table. the asshole tucked some money into one of the whores g-strings & pinched her nipple, & all the while his buddies are there laffing because its a batchelor party & this is the shit you do @ a batchelor party, laffing @ that fucking asshole who is disrespecting my sister & bringing shame to my family. i asked her later on where he was that nite & she said he went "bowling with his friends" which she didn't mind because she wanted some time to relax and hang w/ her girlfriends. And she said it with that attitude of hers like she knows everything & her boyfriend is not out doing things behind her back that make her look like a stupid bitch to everyone who sees.

something in me snapped when i saw him touching that girls tit, i went fucking ~~bollistick~~ belistic. i went up to him & punched his fucking stupid face & knocked him down. him & his buds jumped me but then my crew jumped them & before u knew it we were all thrown out by a bunch of owners, bouncers, etc. & my buddy who was getting married got pissed at <u>me</u>!

u would think the scumbag would learn his lesson but a few weeks later i am in the dewdrop inn. i come back from taking a leak & i see him standing there, standing too close & flirting with some fucking bitch, a girl who KNOWS my sister & was friends with her in high school, & now shes fucking flirting with her friends ~~fiancey~~ fiansay, i actually liked the stupid bitch at one point, but no, she thought she was too good for me. & she is even engaged too, ive heard, so she deserves this just as much as he does.

so i go nuts again. i catch up to him in the parking lot & throw a punch, it was a good punch but hes fast so it didnt land right. so i jumped on him and i would have killed the mother-fucker, all I needed was a few more seconds. but he got away, i guess i just didnt fight dirty enough.

then the asshole goes & tells my sister i attacked him for no reason, he was just standing around talking to gina, that girl they knew from high school, & I went apeshit on him. so then she goes & takes his side, tells me im crazy, what the fuck am i doing, that is the man she is going to marry & we better start getting along better, if i dont cut the shit she is going to kick me out of the wedding party etc. i don't give a shit, i don't want to be in the fucking wedding party, i dont want to cellebrate her getting married to this prick who is going to fuck around on her & end up with a "gooma" while my sister is home trying to keep the house clean & raise kids, the way my mother did (but my father never fucked around on my mother & NEVER WOULD if he lived to be 1 million yrs old).

so i ask her why she lets him go to "lacee's" & "city lites" & the dewdrop inn without her & she said doesnt care, she doesnt have a problem with it, she trusts him & why shouldnt he have a nite out with his friends once in a while, when she just wants to stay home or hang with her girlfriends, everyone knows everyone else at those clubs anyway. i tell her how he was flirting with that putana gina romeo at the inn & she says gina & rog grew up 2 houses from each other, theyve been friends since they were kids. & i say well they must be very good friends because he practically had his finger up her pussy the whole time & she was leaning into him like she was ready to fuck any second. at which point my sister again takes his side & tells me i dont know what the fuck i am talking about, i am the one with the fucking problem & i need glasses because i dont see right.

i never liked that asshole, never. always thought he was hot shit from the time we were in grade school, mr fucking "first baseman" on the baseball field & mr fucking "home run king" in the bedroom or the backseat of his corvette which he thought was so cool. mr "king of the prom" & good time guy @ the shore, thinking he was so smoothe with the ladies & fucking like a rabbit. never gave me the time of day & all of a sudden when he starts dateing my sister he starts being "nice" & thinks everything will be forgotten. he was a phoney in high school, even flirting with the teachers & charming his way out of detention, assemblys, etc., & he's still a phoney now, thinks he can just smile & every female heart will melt.

he buys my sister nice things & spends his money & for that reason she thinks hes a good guy, a gennerous guy, a nice guy. its all an act, i know guys who work with him & they say he sucks up to the boss & doesnt work that hard, in fact hes always goofing off when he should be working. so hes a phoney @ work too, like everywhere else. meanwhile i work my ass off in school trying to get an education and work all day & nite at a deli and make zero

$$, and he has some union job where hes on easy street and makes $$$ for doing jackshit all day long. and thats the way the world works, handing everything to roger borelli on a silver platter while the rest of us work and work and get nothing.

he will marry my sister over my dead body. but shes not going to change her mind. & thats where u come in. i feel lucky i saw that ad in the paper, people who eat at the deli are always leaving newspapers behind and boy did that turn out to be lucky for me.

rog has alot of friends so it is going to be tuff to find him alone. DO NOT do this when my sister is anywhere near him. my sister is tall, has long blond hair & a small birthmark on her rt. cheek. she drives a red monte carlo. DO NOT go near his house if u see her car in the driveway or parked on the street near his apt. u MUST do this when I am @ work, which is between noon & 9 pm, mondays thru fridays, or between 7 in the morning & 4 in the afternoon on saturdays. this HAS TO HAPPEN when i am @ work, so that no one gets ~~suspicious~~ susspicious of me. you can also do it on a saturday or sunday nite as i will make sure i am always around plenty of people for the next few months.

i am following directions & signing my name as

C

A

Our Circle of Five is complete. It is time to begin Phase Four.

Before you act, it is imperative that you research your assignment fully. The letter you received should have provided the information you need. However, there is no substitute for extended personal observation.

You now have up to three months to conduct your investigation. Choose your methods carefully. Observe from a distance or get up close and personal, depending on how you wish to proceed. Some suggestions as you move forward:

- Disguise yourself. Men: Grow or shave facial hair. Women: Wear wigs. *Do not* disguise yourself outlandishly. The goal is to blend in, not stand out.
- Dress in a manner different than your normal style. Again, stay within the boundaries of good taste and do not dress in a manner that will attract undue attention.
- Do not allow your own automobile, or other personal vehicle with identifying marks, to be seen while you conduct your research. This is especially important if your vehicle is easily recognizable.
- Be extremely discreet when asking other people for information about the person you are researching.
- *Do not rush.* Do not attempt to collect all the information you need in a short period of time. Asking too many questions in a concentrated onslaught will attract attention, as

will your continued, unexpected, or sudden presence in places you do not normally frequent. *Be patient.*

• Commit to memory any information you receive. Do not keep paper or computerized records of the information.

At the end of your research period, contact me at the P.O. box number I will send to you under separate cover two weeks from now. In the envelope include only a 3" x 5" index card on which you've written a checkmark with a magic marker of the color you've been assigned. As always, *do not* touch the envelope, postage, or index card with your bare hands.

Further instructions will follow when your investigations are complete. Remember: *Be patient,* both in your research and as you wait to hear from me again.

.

D

Orange, Blue

I'm still not convinced this is real, that any of it is going to happen, or that any of it will be followed through on, but I'm desperate enough, so here goes.

Before I get started, though, I have to admit that I wonder whom you have targeted as your "chosen." It would be somehow appropriate if I ended up with your person and you ended up with mine, making our relationship more of a two-way line than the "circle" A keeps talking about.

Since I decided to go through with this, I've been doing a lot of thinking about what might drive other people to these acts of desperation. Is your tale one of sordid trailer park lust and jealousy? Maybe you were spurned by someone, and this is your way of getting his or her attention once and for all? Were you jilted by a lover, betrayed by a friend, or robbed by a business associate? Did a bully in your childhood pick on you, or does a bully in your adult life push you around now? Did someone take advantage of your good nature, hurt your children, or mistreat your parents? Do you have a rival or competitor whose elimination will lead to your progress, advancement, or wealth? Do you have hostilities towards people of specific races, genders, sexualities, or ethnicities?

My hunch is that your hostility, like all hostility, is probably petty and small-minded, that you've been slighted somehow and are looking for revenge. But I'm not here to judge. Certainly I have no right to do that, because I have turned to exactly the same method of dealing with my issue.

I do want you to know, though, that the person whose acquaintance you'll be making (briefly, fleetingly) is not an ex-lover of mine, not someone who stole a boyfriend from me, and not an ex-husband who used the court system to rob me of my children. In short, my motives are noble. What I'm doing, I am doing for the good of society.

The best analogy I can draw is this: Suppose that, before 9/11, you gazed into a crystal ball and saw what would happen to the Twin Towers. Also suppose that, for some reason, you had the opportunity to assassinate Osama Bin Laden one evening in a Kabul alleyway. Having looked into that crystal ball, would you hesitate *in the least* to pull the trigger? Of course you would not. You'd know you were ridding the world of a force so malicious, so evil, so unrepentant that you'd feel no remorse. Instead of feeling guilty, you'd congratulate yourself for taking firm, decisive action while you had the opportunity.

The truth is, my "chosen" is not someone who has hurt me directly. But half a decade of working near him, and seeing the results of his horrific prejudice, racism, and sexism, have convinced me that he must be removed before he can do any further damage.

His name is Dr. John Althorp, and he is Dean of Humanities at Mendham College in New Rochelle, New York. His office phone number is 914-■■■-2200, extension ■■■■. He lives in a high-rise condo on the Hudson River in Riverdale, NY. The address is 4580 ■■■■■■■■■■ Avenue, Apt. 12F, Riverdale (not "Bronx"—that would be too lowbrow for him), NY 10471. His phone number there is 718-■■■-9867.

My acquaintance with Dr. Althorp began slightly more than five years ago, when he was Chair of Mendham's English and

Rhetoric Department. I'd taken my Ph.D. a year earlier from a Midwestern university and had been actively looking for a full-time, tenure-track position at a liberal arts college. I'd interviewed—well—with some of the more progressive programs in Idaho, Nebraska, and Kansas. But I was born and raised in New York City, and after graduate school I wanted to return here.

And I'm sure you can imagine why. I don't know if you've spent much time in the Midwest, but outside the university towns, the entire area is a vast, desolate wasteland void of culture. Certainly there are no arty or culturally aware newspapers like *The Clarion*, in which I found A's advertisement. This may sound somewhat snobbish—and I really don't mean to be snooty—but there's no denying that the middle part of the country is much less advanced in terms of attitudes and lifestyles than the coasts. I'd had a fellowship with a generous stipend from my Ph.D. program, which is one of the top ten in the country, so—if you know anything at all about graduate studies in literature and gender—you know that I couldn't pass up the opportunity to study with some of the foremost literary theorists, even though I'd be doing so in the middle of nowhere. But by the time my dissertation was accepted, I'd had enough of the Midwest, and I didn't want to spend the next decade of my life teaching at some second-rate school in Idaho, Kansas, or Nebraska. I wanted to come back to New York, though I would have settled for Connecticut, New Jersey, or Philadelphia, any of which would have allowed me easy access to the City.

As the result of an impending retirement around that time, Mendham College was conducting a search for a Ph.D. to teach literature of the Victorian period, early drama, and of course the dreaded first-year composition courses. The job seemed like the perfect fit in so many ways. I'd done my dissertation on gender-identity crisis in the works of George Eliot and had studied under some of the preeminent Victorian scholars. In addition, I'd done my oral exams on pre-Shakespearean drama and had begun doing some exploratory work on gender role reversal in the early plays. As for the freshman comp courses, they are the crosses that college English professors have to bear—the classes in which overqualified Ph.D's make futile attempts to get uninterested, unevolved, alcohol-happy freshmen to write a decent essay. There's simply no way around the comp courses until you're a full professor who's been tenured for twenty years and teaches only graduate students, so young profs grit their teeth, suffer through 101 and 102, and live for their beloved 325 and 408.

Having grown up in the City, I'd heard of Mendham College, but I didn't know much about it. As it turned out, the school was founded in the late 1800s and is housed on quite a lovely fifty-acre campus filled with trees, flowers, and nature walks that are open to the public. Through friends and colleagues I'd met at conventions, in graduate school, or via listservs, newsgroups, and other Internet academic communities, I pieced together the inside story on Mendham. The pros: New York location, decent starting salary, good benefits, reasonable teaching load (three courses per semester), release time for research, reasonable committee requirements. The cons: the cost of living, the student body (mostly blue collar), the relative obscurity of the school (which had a decent reputation, but didn't garner any sort of instant recognition or respect in academic circles).

On balance, the pros seemed to outweigh the cons. I'd learned to live frugally in grad school, so setting myself up on the generous (by academic standards) $35,000 assistant professor salary seemed doable. And the school's obscurity could be a benefit, in a way. The top administrators at such schools are always uptight that the school doesn't get more recognition or have more prestige, and a young, up-and-coming academic can play on that insecurity to get more release time for research. As for the student body—well, I've never been interested in teaching anyone but the best and brightest. I knew I'd be able to reach those who were interested and intellectually curious. I'd give the rest of them C's, and none of them would care.

The largest problem, and the one that would be the most difficult to surmount, was the school's reputation for being traditional. A journey through the course catalog showed exactly what "traditional" meant: a slew of survey courses through the literary "periods," a series of genre-based courses, and a few electives. Almost no theory; no women's literature courses; no theme-based courses; nothing daring, experimental, avant-garde, or forward-looking in any way. The textbooks had been in use for decades, and many of the professors were still teaching from their yellowed notes from 1960. Even those who had the rank of full professor hadn't published much more than two or three articles twenty years earlier.

Still, I told myself, there are ways around such things. If you have a cooperative chair, you can pretty much do whatever you want with your syllabus despite what the course catalog promises. So I decided to suspend my worries and sit for the interview.

As I suspected, the faculty were a mixture of the moderately stodgy and the heavily stodgy. They all *said* they were looking forward to the infusion of fresh blood. After all, no new full-time faculty had been hired into the department for more than fifteen years. Underneath the purported enthusiasm, though, I could sense the trepidation. They were set in their ways. They wanted someone who'd fit in and not make waves. A good little boy (preferably) or girl.

I turned on the charm (which is easy to do with overweight white men of a certain age) and impressed the search committee with my knowledge of the literature they'd all been teaching the same way for thirty years. They were also delighted by the almost perfect match between my scholarly background and their needs. All of them pointed out the difficulty of finding someone equally expert in Victorian lit and early drama, as I am; the retiring professor (male, of course—the only woman in the department was Gretel Liebtrau, a decent, if not stellar, researcher/scholar who has become a bit of an ally) had been somewhat of a Renaissance man with two Ph.D.'s, one in each area. I met him, too, and found him to be far and away the most impressive faculty member in terms of knowledge and intellect. He'd gotten fat and comfortable, like the rest of them, but his scholarly light shined throughout our conversation.

To my surprise, I was offered the job. Changing times had worked in my favor. Later on I heard through the grapevine that the board of directors, as well as the Dean and the Provost, had pressured the hiring committee to choose a woman. It was a new millennium, after all. Mendham's faculty were still overwhelmingly male at the time, and the world—along with the tuition-paying students and their parents—had begun to take notice.

I also discovered, much later, that Dr. Althorp had vehemently opposed my hiring. My spies told me he'd called me "two-faced," "phony," and "haughty," then predicted I'd be "the biggest troublemaker this campus has ever seen." But throughout the interview he'd smiled and talked pleasantly, and I'd left thinking of him as a nice, if not particularly interesting or brilliant, man. It was only a matter of time before he showed his true colors, but more on that later.

I simply couldn't turn down the job. Tenure-track positions in or near New York are practically impossible to find. If I hadn't accepted the offer, it could have been years before a similar opportunity opened up, and I didn't want to relegate myself to adjunct work at Columbia or NYU, which would keep me living at or below the poverty line. And I was still young. Mendham College need not be forever. I'd need to publish and present many papers, write a few books, and attend many, many meetings of the Modern Language Association before making the jump to a top-tier school, of course, but I was confident I'd make that leap after eight or nine years of hard work, at which point I'd still be quite energetic. So I accepted the position and moved back East.

For the most part, Dr. Althorp and I coexisted peacefully for the two years he continued as Chair, before he was promoted to Dean. And to this day we still officially "get along." Despite our many differences, there are no open hostilities, no screaming matches, no daily dramas. But over the last several years, I've watched John make one offensive, mean-spirited decision after another. And it's the cumulative effect of all those decisions that has brought me to where I stand now: considering him a malignant presence not only on the campus but in society at large. John Althorp isn't a huge, open, festering sore that everyone can see. He is a quiet cancer—a disease all the more insidious because the destruction it wreaks is nearly complete before it's ever detected.

So what, exactly, has John Althorp done to warrant his fate? I can't possibly recount all the stories, but here are a few. Despite majority support for the idea, he has steadfastly refused to approve the addition of any women's literature courses to the curriculum. His official "reason" is that women's literature should be integrated into the existing canon, and that more women writers should be placed into the existing courses of a "well-established and highly respected curriculum" (his words). In the last two years, two full-time positions in the English department have opened up. Both have gone to white men, despite the fact that many better-qualified women had applied for both positions. John always has a glib explanation, usually in the "delightful person, amazing scholar, but not a good fit for Mendham" category.

When I could no longer ignore the mounting evidence, I began making discreet inquiries about the experiences other faculty and staff have had with him. I have a following among some of the female students, many of whom have reported unpleasant encounters, with uncomfortable sexual overtones, with Dean Althorp (who still teaches one literature course per semester). It seems that Dean Althorp is quite a willing admirer of large breasts and shapely legs, and he doesn't always avert his eyes when he should. However, his admiration for women hasn't led him to advocate for them in any way; he's been instrumental, I've found out, in diverting much-needed funding for women's sports into the men's teams. The men's basketball team gets highly-paid coaches and expensive equipment; the women's team gets inexperienced coaches and leftover supplies from the men's team.

Acting on some leads and with the help of an ally in the transcript department, I made a few other discoveries as well. Would it surprise you to learn that, over the years, African-American, Asian-American, and Latina/Latino students have consistently received lower grades from Dr. Althorp than white students of European background? In my time at Mendham, I've had many a bright, hard-working minority student come to me in tears, showing me a well-written, cogently argued paper s/he'd prepared for Dr. Althorp, only to receive a C or C-minus for her or his efforts. Those same students received much less attention in class, and you can be sure none of them were included in the "field trips" that Dr. Althorp schedules with his favorites. In his tenure as Dean, he's supervised the hiring of more than three dozen new faculty. Only three of the hires have been people of color, and only six of them have been women. In this day and age, in one of the most diverse areas of the country, this sort of behavior must not be allowed to continue.

It won't shock you to know that Dr. Althorp has also been a vocal critic of race-based admissions and affirmative action policies, despite the Ann Arbor ruling of a few years back. He's firmly opposed to allowing the college to offer the remedial courses in English and math so often needed by minority students to give them a fair chance at succeeding in college and in life. He serves as moderator of the Young Republicans Club and has allowed Pro-Choice demonstrations on campus—in the name of "free speech," he says. He has opposed the faculty union movement. Just last week, he complimented me on the publication of my recent book (with a prestigious university press), then muttered to another faculty member, "So this is what the study of literature is coming to? The woman can't write, she makes no sense, she's a blowhard who doesn't know what she's talking about." Well, I think you can see from this letter that I *do* know how to write, I'm *not* a blowhard, and I *do* know what I'm talking about.

You know, this country still has a *long* way to go in a lot of areas, but the progress we've made in the last couple of decades has been miraculous, if you consider where we've been. We should be looking to the leaders of our nation's educational system to lead the charge in wiping out the many inequities that remain. Isn't this goal, or shouldn't this goal be, the basis for all studies in the humanities, of which John Althorp is the dean?

Yes, it should be. But we're not going to get to where we need to be when people like John Althorp remain in positions of power. And John Althorp isn't going anywhere. He's tenured, and he has many allies. He's still fairly young and has no plans to retire any time soon. If anything, his ambitions will only take him higher in the college's administration, where he'll be able to hold back progress even more.

John's office hours are officially 9 a.m. to 4 p.m., Monday to Friday. As an administrator, though, he is frequently at meetings, and his secretary (who loathes him, I can assure you) serves as gatekeeper when he *is* in his office. The secretary (Marianne Peters) leaves at 3 each day, so you may have a window of opportunity between 3 and 4 p.m. However, I'd ask that you *not* take care of this on campus. The effects would be quite harmful to Mendham's reputation, I think, and I don't want to see the school suffer for the sins of its Dean.

I don't know much about John's life off campus. I gave you his address earlier; I've confirmed it (discreetly, of course), so I know it's correct, but I've never been to his place so I can't tell you anything about the building or neighborhood. I *can* tell you, however, that he drives a late-model black Mercedes sedan, NY license plate ▆▆▆▆ ▆▆▆, with an oval UK sticker on the right side of the rear bumper. (Interesting how much money the administrators make in comparison to the faculty, isn't it?) I've seen him eating at a few local places for lunch (Tiger's Deli and Hothouse Harry's on Main Street in New Rochelle), usually in the company of his administrator cronies. The enclosed photo is from last year's yearbook and is quite an accurate portrait of the man.

I do know that he's married; I've met his wife a couple of times. She didn't make much of an impression on me, but she seems like a downtrodden woman. I hope he has a big life insurance policy that will allow her to live it up when he's gone. He has two kids, both girls, both away at college. Can you blame them for wanting to get away from their father?

Please don't do anything to harm the wife or children.

Oh, also, he plays golf (surprise, surprise) at the Valhalla Country Club with the Provost on weekends. Photos of him in his ridiculous golf clothes adorn the walls of his office (which, needless to say, is about six times the size of mine).

I realize there is some rancor in this letter, but even though I detest the man I do hope you'll do this as quickly and painlessly as possible. While it's certainly in the world's best interests to chop this malignant growth off the tree, I don't want him to suffer needlessly.

I know we will never meet, which is a good thing, but I hope you're African-American, or Asian-American, or Latino, or queer, or female. That would be true poetic justice.

A

Your research is complete.

It is now time to move into the final phase. You know what you have to do. Now is the time to decide when, where, and how you will do it.

Do not rush into anything when you receive this letter. My assumption is that your various assignments are geographically dispersed enough not to call undue attention to our Circle's activities. However, a cluster of mishaps over too short a period of time may raise eyebrows and cause those in law enforcement with too much time on their hands to begin asking questions and looking for linkages. We have all been extremely cautious in our proceedings up through this point. Continued caution is essential for all of our protection.

That said, only you will know, based on your research, when it is best to proceed. However, I expect that you will carry out your assignment within six months.

A few tips as you move forward:

- Ensure that your vehicle, if you have one, is not located anywhere near the scene, at any time.
- Change your appearance as directed in earlier correspondence.
- If you act on your assignment in that person's home, wear gloves and do not touch anything in the house or apartment. To create a credible blind, you may wish to remove

any cash or easily portable valuables you find. Spend the cash and destroy the other valuables.

The method you use to complete your assignment is up to you. Keep in mind the following pointer, however: Blood is messy, and specks of it can show up in unexpected places. (Think O.J. Simpson and the Bronco.) Avoid knives and razors. Poisons are clean and fast acting (a list of suggestions is enclosed). Guns work well, too. *Do not* touch with your bare hands any weapon you may use, and *destroy* it as soon as possible after the completion of your assignment.

When your assignment is complete, send an envelope to me at the P.O. box number I will provide to you under separate cover. In the envelope, simply include a piece of construction paper of the color you've been assigned. One week later, forward your journal or final report to the same P.O. box. I will then forward your letter, unread, to the person whose chosen you've dispatched.

Due to the double-blind system, I will not be able to notify you when your chosen has been dispatched. Instead, you will hear through the normal channels—newspapers, TV, and so on. It is critical that you maintain calm and remain unemotional when you hear the news. In the unlikely chance that anyone asks you any questions, answer those questions calmly and *do not* volunteer any information. *Do not* talk too much. It is a sign of nervousness, and I can guarantee you that people will notice it.

This has been a long road, but everything is now ready. Best of luck.

.

E

Green & Black

Dear Fellow Murderer:

Ha ha. Sorry for the little joke. This is kind of nerve-wracking, isn't it? A little humor goes a long way and all that, etc.

You're probably thinking, What if this is all a set-up? But don't worry. For reasons I can't go into, I know that it *isn't* a set-up and that it's all real. So instead of looking a gift horse in the mouth, I'm going to count my blessings and just get on with it.

Here is your assignment.

> Joseph Castro
> ■■■-■■ ■■■th Place
> Astoria, NY
> home: 718-■■■-6224.

The photos are recent. I got the first one from Google. The other two come from neighborhood newspapers. They accompanied stories in which Joseph Castro received public recognition and thanks for his many good works in the community.

Joe Castro is twice divorced, no children. He used to live with his wives in the house in Astoria, but they get thrown out when he divorces them. For, you see, Mr. Castro has certain methods at his disposal to ensure that judicial decisions go his way. Thanks to the Freedom of Information Act, I've been able to access the proceedings of his divorce trials. Despite the excellent lawyers retained by his ex-wives and a preponderance of evidence showing beyond a reasonable doubt that Mr. Castro is an adulterer and abuser, he pays no alimony and has no responsibilities to these women.

In fact, Mr. Castro gets away with a lot, much more than the average citizen ever could. He's had speeding tickets dismissed all over the Eastern seaboard (100 miles an hour on the Florida Turnpike, 102 miles an hour on Route 95 in Connecticut, 99 miles an hour on the Long Island Expressway). He's slapped around his lovers (a disciplinary action in which he seems to take great pride, based on conversations he's had with friends), driven intoxicated with impunity, and deprived prostitutes of their income when he's finished with them.

You wouldn't know about this side of Joe Castro from the newspaper articles. He's been most generous with the local Little League and soccer teams, serving as coach of one team and assistant coach of the other. When he isn't drinking for free at a bar whose owner is afraid to charge him for a beer, or eating for free at a restaurant whose proprietor knows better than to charge him for a meal, he volunteers his time to visit grammar schools, where he talks about the evils of alcohol and drug abuse, then has photos taken with the children he's just saved from substance addiction. One night last spring, while he was sleeping soundly, he heard a car alarm going off down the block. He rushed to the scene in his pajamas and saw a young thug attempting to steal a small Honda. He wrestled the thief to the ground and saved the car, which a devoted son had recently purchased for his widowed mother. Needless to say, Mr. Castro received an outpouring of public love for his selfless act. Letters to the editor commended him, and neighbors threw a block party to celebrate his heroism.

You may be asking yourself: Does this man have a split personality? Is he two people, one good, one evil? Does he deserve what I'm asking you to do? I've asked myself that last question dozens of times. All I can say is this: If I'd answered it differently, you wouldn't be reading this letter right now.

Because, in the simplest possible terms, Mr. Castro is a liar and a hypocrite. He presents one face to the world, that of the goodhearted neighbor and public servant. Only those closest to him know his dark secrets.

I just reread what I've written so far, and I realize the description I've given is likely to give you the impression that Joe Castro is involved in organized crime. How else, you're probably thinking, could he get away with his behavior? Who else could stack judges in his favor? For what other type of person would those in authority repeatedly look the other way?

I'll tell you what other type of person. A police officer.

I debated whether or not to provide you with this information, but I think it's important that you know it. Given his profession, Joe Castro is much better equipped to protect himself than the average person. From the pictures I've enclosed here, you can see he's in exceedingly good physical shape. He lifts weights every day before his duty shift at Astoria Gym and Fitness on ■■■■■■■ Boulevard. The gym is owned by one of his neighbors. Joe has a key to the gym and shows up there around five a.m. The owner usually shows up around six, so you have a one-hour window of opportunity in the morning. (I doubt Joe carries his gun with him while he's lifting weights, but I'm guessing it's probably within his reach most other times.)

He also moonlights as a bouncer at ■■■■■■■ Night Club in Brooklyn (138 ■■■■■■ Street) on weekends. I've called the club and inquired about its hours. Its doors open at 10 p.m., and the place closes at 4 a.m. Joe usually arrives there slightly before the club opens and leaves for home (often with a woman) shortly after it closes. He's also told me that if he doesn't have any luck picking up a whore (his words) at the club, he'll sometimes drive into Manhattan to find one of the prostitutes he shakes down. Needless to say, I don't recommend doing this in Manhattan (too many people around at all hours of the day and night).

He drives an unmarked New York City police car while he's on duty. Off duty he drives a Harley-Davidson motorcycle (NY license ■■■■■■■) or a red Jeep Wrangler, NY license plate ■■■ ■■■■. I've seen him on the motorcycle only on the weekends, when he gets dressed up in leather and, I've heard, drives upstate, sometimes by himself, sometimes with a group of similarly clad Weekend Warriors.

He usually attends mass at St. Elizabeth's Roman Catholic Church in Astoria on Sundays at 11 a.m. I don't bring this up because I think his attendance at mass provides a good opportunity for you to do your job. Exactly the opposite, actually. I would never want anything to happen to him in or near the church, where so many families are engaged in worship or other community activities. So please, anywhere but the church grounds.

I suppose before I end this letter, I need to justify the action I'm taking by sending it to you. I've searched deep within myself, and within the Bible, to figure out whether I'm doing the right thing. Jesus clearly stated, "Judge not, lest ye be judged." And who am I to stand in judgment of Joe Castro? From one perspective, he is a disturbed, unhappy man who will get what he deserves when he passes from this earth.

But the Old Testament clearly states "an eye for an eye, and a tooth for a tooth." Something needs to be done about the many eyes Joe Castro has gouged, and the many teeth he has pulled out, while masquerading as a civil servant. His evil shows no sign of abating. In fact, he is getting worse—more malicious, more greedy, more hypocritical. Under normal circumstances, society would do something to remove him from our midst. But in this case, society cannot protect its own best interests, because many of those in charge of protecting the public are as corrupt as Joe Castro himself. And so Joe Castro is free to continue exploiting and abusing those around him with impunity.

Until now, that is.

I've made my peace with this decision. It is the right thing to do. May God bless you in your efforts.

A

I'm 100% ready for my assignment. I hope you're ready for yours, too.

Here's the basic information you need. The man's real name is Jesse Garanowicz, though he has gone by a bunch of other names: Topher Smith, Chip Garran, and Greg Meyers. Each time he gets found out and moves, he changes his name and appearance. When he lived in Pennsylvania, he had a blond crew cut and a permanent tan. Both of them came out of bottles. When he fled to Jersey, he let his hair grow out until it was long, stringy, and its natural brown. Now that he's in Brooklyn, he's gotten a perm and sports a fashionable trace beard to hide his acne scars.

Photos of him in each of these guises are enclosed. The most recent one is the picture with the curly hair and trace beard, taken just a few days ago by a hidden camera. The other pics are included just in case he decides to undergo another transformation, so that you can get a sense of how he might look. With the double-blind system that our Circle is working under, I won't be able to send you any updated pics, because no one knows who is receiving this letter (not even me).

Let me tell you more about Jesse Garanowicz.

He was born Buckingham, PA, a distant suburb of Philadelphia. If you talked to neighbors, teachers, or schoolmates (not friends, because he's never had any), they'd tell you Jesse was always a little strange. He was quiet and kept to himself. When the bullies beat up on skinny little Jesse, he took it like a man and went home to lick his wounds.

Jesse molested his first little girl when he was twelve years old. Jesse's mother came home to find that her son had tied up a neighbor's five-year-old daughter and was busy manipulating various parts of her anatomy with a butter knife. Fortunately for Jesse, the Garanowiczes were well-to-do. The father was involved in politics, and the mother was a fixture in The Women's League of Buckingham, so the unpleasant incident was hushed up.

When Jesse was fifteen, he used a brick to knock the paper-boy unconscious, then raped him. When Jesse was sixteen, he dragged the daughter of the high school custodian into the boys' room and held her head in the toilet while he penetrated her from behind. When he was seventeen, he kidnapped twin six-year-old girls whom their nanny had left unattended for "just a second." This time, he was caught in the act. A watchful neighbor called the police when she saw skinny, but Satanically strong, 105-pound Jesse dragging the sack of struggling girls across the backyard of his house and into the basement.

Mr. and Mrs. Garanowicz swore on a stack of Bibles that their boy would never do the horrible things he was accused of. Highly respected and equally highly paid doctors testified in Jesse's defense, arguing that he was mentally ill and needed treatment. And one look at Jesse was enough to convince you that Jesse wouldn't hurt a fly. Those big sad eyes! That sweet smile! And how could anyone that fragile-looking be a threat to anyone?

Still, something had to be done, and Jesse was sentenced to fifteen years in a Pennsylvania institute for sex offenders. His progress was not good. Not surprising, since these sick assholes never "get better," despite what bleeding heart liberals want everyone to believe.

And then, in the blink of an eye, Jesse's fifteen-year sentence had been served. Jesse was 33 years old and ready to be released.

One of Jesse's doctors/psychiatrists attempted to intercede. She filed a frantic report and made phone calls to people in high places. Jesse shouldn't be allowed out yet, she said. If he was, she continued, there was a 100% chance that he would rape another child. See, it seems that Jesse had talked to Dr. Cook about his recurrent fantasies of raping and murdering children, fantasies that hadn't abated much during his fifteen years of "therapy."

If you or I had been in charge, would we have let Jesse Garanowicz out on the streets to rape another kid? Of course we wouldn't have. But this is America, where we protect the guilty and punish the victims. The judge (some said he was a drinking buddy of Mr. Garanowicz) ruled that Jesse had served his time, had *paid his debt to society*, and was free to go.

The media got hold of it, and an uproar followed. For about six months, the U.S. government provided poor defenseless Jesse with 24-hour protection against those who might wish him harm. Meanwhile, Mr. and Mrs. Garanowicz received angry phone calls and hate mail daily, along with threats to burn down their house if they continued to harbor a pervert. The parents couldn't take the stress. Mr. G. had a heart attack and died at home, at which point Mrs. G. sold the house and moved to a retirement villa in Florida.

Rumor had it that Mrs. G. made it clear that Jesse was not welcome in her new home. Neighbors speculated that she blamed Jesse for her husband's death and her discouraging loss of status in the community. She gave her son a ton of money and then left him on his own, telling him not to call her, ever again, for any reason.

But Jesse was still the target of mob hatred and couldn't be expected to survive very long on his own. So our cooperative government agencies quietly found him a place to live in an urban area in southern New Jersey. They also found him a job in a factory and offered continued counseling to help him control his problematic urges.

Jesse wanted to start afresh. So he changed his hairstyle, packed his things, and moved to South Jersey.

The Pennsylvania mob lost track of Jesse. As long as he was out of their state, they couldn't have cared less where he'd gone. Jesse was on good behavior his first year in Jersey, keeping his hands to himself while he amassed a collection of child pornography. Through the marvels of the Internet, he made contact with a group of other twisted freaks, and they exchanged photos, contraband videos, and erotic stories of their former and future seductions/murders.

Within two years, two children from South Jersey (a five-year-old boy and a six-year-old girl) disappeared. Police questioned Jesse, but there was no evidence to link him to the disappearances. The kids were never found, but four years later the FBI found pictures of their dead, naked bodies in Jesse's ample collection.

The police in South Jersey knew who'd killed those kids, but Jesse had covered his tracks well. He was brought in for questioning, but prosecutors couldn't find the evidence they needed to convict him. According to the laws of this great country, pornographic photos are just "circumstantial" evidence, and the fact that you like to look at pictures of naked children doesn't mean you also like to murder them.

And then a glorious thing happened, something that probably saved the lives of at least five more South Jersey kids. In the wake of a horrible child sex killing in Hamilton, NJ, the state legislature passed "Megan's Law," which requires New Jersey communities to notify residents of convicted pedophiles living among them. Jesse had been watching the story closely. The second the law passed, he was on his way out of New Jersey and into Brooklyn. It was time for another change of appearance, too.

Jesse has been living in a Brooklyn high rise for ten years now. In those years, the police know about three attempted child snatchings, all in Queens, that fit Jesse's M.O. All three times, the kids got away, and on two occasions the kids' caretakers saw the man who'd been enticing the children. Both caretakers picked Jesse out from a line-up.

But the legal system being what is, Jesse walked scott free both times. There wasn't enough evidence at trial, and a good defense attorney (financed, rumor has it, by the money his mother had given him years earlier) was able to raise reasonable doubt in the juries' minds.

Three months ago, a child disappeared from a park near his building in Astoria, Queens. The poor troubled kid had had a fight with his stepfather and run out of the apartment, and he'd been walking around the park when a man approached him. Eyewitnesses saw him leave with a man whose description matched that of Jesse Garanowicz. The boy hasn't been seen since.

Jesse remains untouchable. He doesn't have an alibi, but he's learned his trade well. There are no traces of the boy in Jesse's apartment, in his car, or on his clothes. No DNA, no fibers, no blood, no nothing. Each time the police bring him in for questioning, they're forced to let him go. Meanwhile, this sick fuck continues to destroy lives while living in the comfort of a luxury apartment that 99% of the people in this city couldn't afford.

So you can see why I am resorting to this unorthodox method of dealing with Mr. Garanowicz. If the police and the other people in authority can't stop this monster, we can. That's where you come in.

I've been referring to him as "Jesse Garanowicz" throughout this letter, because that is his real name. He knows better than to go by it, though. The name you'll find him using now is Teddy Boyle.

You'll find him living at 133 ■■■■■■■■■ Street in Brooklyn Heights. Apartment 1215. 718-■■■-4310. I've included several maps with this letter, showing driving directions from within NYC and from New Jersey, Connecticut, and other points in the tri-state area. Subway directions are also enclosed in case you don't have a car.

133 ■■■■■■■■■ Street is a secured building with a 24-hour doorman and a single security camera in the lobby. So you'll need to be very, very careful. Disguise your identity closely if you enter through the front doors. A better way to enter may be through the garage. Residents have an automatic garage door opener that leads to an underground garage in the front of the building. You may be able to slip in that way, but remember, there are cameras there, too. The laundry room on the ground floor has an exit directly out of the building into the rear playground, but you can enter the building only if you catch someone who is going out at the time you're trying to get in.

Jesse/Teddy doesn't go out much, except for road trips to odd locations every few months. He doesn't have a job. A few times a week he strolls a couple of blocks to Vito's Deli on ■■■■■■ Street (see map). He belongs to the video store at 54 ■■■■■■■■ Street (again, see map) and shops at the Key Foods on ■■■■■ Street (map). Depending on how much he's buying he either walks to the supermarket or drives.

His car is a beat-up old white 1978 Honda Civic hatchback, license plate BFP ■■■■. Here's how I remember it: BFP stands for Big Fucking Pedophile.

Don't let Jesse's size fool you. You'd be amazed at how strong the insane can be. The only way you're going to get Jesse is to surprise him. So do it quick and then get out.

One thing working in your favor is that Jesse doesn't seem to have any weapons (firearms, that is). I've done my research here, and he's never used such a weapon in any of his abductions, which makes me think he doesn't have any. I could be wrong, but I don't think I am.

I can't touch this guy; I'm too closely involved with him at this point to get away with it. But you can do what I can't. I know you'll stand strong and do what has to be done. I can't lose another child to Jesse Garanowicz.

Part 2

Betty Lewis
(B)

Dear Nicholas,

Hello, my dear. I haven't heard from you in a while, so I'm dropping you an e-mail to make sure you're still alive and well. From what I've been hearing, young people today check their e-mail constantly, and I thought this might be a more effective way of getting in touch, rather than leaving those long-winded messages on your answering machine. And to be honest, I actually have come to quite like e-mail and the Internet. Of course I was a bit intimidated when everything went computerized at work, but what was I going to do, retire? I can't afford that, so I made myself keep up with the times, and I'm glad I did.

Anyway—I know your job is exhausting, which is why you can't be in touch more often, but I would so appreciate a quick e-mail or call, even if only for a minute once a month, to let me know you are OK and happy. Though I can't imagine how anyone could be happy doing the job you do. I don't say that in a judgmental way, but more out of concern. I want you to have what I didn't have—a wife, children, a reliable support network— and I fear that your profession is making it tough for you to make all that happen. Speaking as a single woman (though one who is three-plus decades your senior) I can tell you, I would definitely think twice if a man in your position were to ask me out. I'm not sure I could deal with the worry of whether or not you'd come home at night, or if I'd get a call one day summoning me to the morgue to identify your body.

How are things looking for your promotion? Any news yet? The suspense is taking a few years off my life, I think—and I fear I am confusing God in the process. Some nights I pray you get the job you want and deserve. You've certainly labored hard enough, giving up a decade of your life, doing work that can get you killed at any minute. Other nights I pray you won't get promoted, so that you'll get angry and quit and do something safe and steady, like work for a bank or insurance company. As I've said before, there's no shame in insurance. Everyone needs it, and the profits are always (and I do mean *always*) good, which means a steady job and vacation time. The Manhattan Mutual Life Insurance Company supported me and Mother for many years, and when I finally retire they'll give me a decent pension, too. I know you can take early retirement from the force and get a pension, too, but the question is: Will you be alive to enjoy either one of them?

That's a serious question, Nicholas. I look around me and I can't believe how everything in society is heading in the wrong direction. Television is basically a medium for depravity and perversion. Radio is filled with disc jockeys whose language would have made sailors from my time blush. Magazines are one step away from pornography. And nobody speaks English any more. It seems that every store in downtown Bloomfield is owned by foreigners who jabber in their language and make you feel uncomfortable when you walk in. The Orientals who run the dry cleaners don't look at you, don't make conversation, and take your money without saying a word. The Hindus who own the convenience store listen to their crazy music and overcharge for everything, yammering on their cell phones when they should be wishing you a good day—the way old Mr. Bertram used to at the candy store on West 230th Street when I was a girl. I've stopped going to the Hindu store. It just isn't clean, and the people who work there smell dirty, and I'm going to start looking for a new dry cleaner, too. I respect the rights of immigrants to come to this country and make an honest living, but they don't have the right to treat me with the bare minimum of respect and then expect me to keep coming back, giving them the money I've worked so hard to earn.

And you know, everyone on my street feels the same way. Somehow, miraculously, ■■■■ ■■■■■■■ Road still manages to feel like life the way it used to be. Why must everything these days be based on politically correct posturing rather than the reality everyone knows exists? What's wrong with wanting to live among people who share a similar background, the same world view, and a similar set of values? The reason this neighborhood is so stable and safe is that it was settled by people who all wanted the same things. Just about all of us moved here to escape from the City, or from various parts of New Jersey that started to become slums in the 60s (especially Newark—a really dangerous place these days, as I'm sure you know, and only getting worse, if you ask me—despite all my tax dollars being poured into "reinvigorating" a city that is basically dead, except for an ugly airport that people pass through on their way to somewhere else). We like things the way they are, and we don't want change forced on us.

But I wonder how much longer we can hold out. A Hispanic couple bought the house at the start of the block, and already I'm seeing the effects. The father can speak English, but the mother, who seems nice enough, just smiles and nods. Meanwhile I hear her speaking Spanish to the kids, and the children speaking Spanish back to her. She's living in this country—why isn't she learning English? She's a young woman, for God's sake, maybe 30 at the oldest. I'm afraid what's going to happen when the summer comes. Will they be hosting wild parties, with loud music and dozens of relatives, and disturbing our peace? I certainly hope not, but I can tell you, several of us have already made a pact to call the police the first time something like that happens so that we can nip any bad behavior in the bud.

Not that we've had a lot of luck in that regard lately. The situation a few doors down has gone from bad to worse. It is so obvious that he's selling drugs, but no one does anything about it. Why, Nick? Please tell me why. I wish you lived in New Jersey so you could help, because the police here really don't seem that concerned about it. The officer who was here the other day actually said to me, "Mrs. Lewis, why don't you just try ignoring him for a while? He's a trouble maker, and all this attention is just provoking him. Lay off him for a while, let him die of a drug overdose in his house, and you'll be free of him soon enough."

Can you believe it? A man paid to enforce the law basically admitted to me that a drug dealer lives four doors away from me, and there is nothing he is going to do about it. And this is what I mean about the way things have changed. I wish you could have seen the Bronx in the old days—so clean and well kept, even pretty on the Concourse and Broadway, but more than that, a place where the neighborhood men banded together to make sure the undesirables stayed out. Now, fifty years later, a drug dealer moves into your neighborhood and the police tell you to mind your own business. I wish you could help more with this situation, Nick, I really do.

Forgive me for venting...I am just so frustrated. I never intended to become a crotchety old woman, like Mother during her last few years. I admit her attitude vexed me quite a bit at the time, and I vowed I'd never become as contrary and difficult as she became. But now I understand better. When you have no control, you fight back however you can. Mother fought back by lashing out, by becoming demanding and bitter. By the end, she'd come to hate the Bronx so much that I had to move her out of her bedroom and into mine. Hers had looked out on what had once been a playground where I'd see-sawed and played hopscotch as a girl. It had become a pit of broken asphalt, used condoms, and drug vials, and she couldn't look out her window without devolving into a profanity-filled rage. My bedroom at least looked out on the street, and while the graffiti there was as much a symbol of the Bronx's downslide as the broken swing set out back, it didn't seem to set Mother off quite as much, or as often.

I wish I'd known about her money. If I had, I could have helped you when you needed help. I also could have moved us to this house a lot sooner, since I had control over what I thought were her limited finances the last few years of her life. She would have enjoyed spending her last few years in a house in the suburbs, I think, with a backyard and a garden and birds chirping in the morning. She would have enjoyed looking out her bedroom window at the lovely stand of elm and oak trees that drop more leaves than any human being can imagine in the autumn. She would have appreciated the peace and quiet she'd been looking for her entire life.

But she would have brought her history, her personality, and her demands with her to ■■■■ ■■■■■■■ Road, too. I'd lived with Mother, and done her chores and her bidding and her errands, for six decades. I'd supported her for almost twenty years. And the house in the suburbs was much more my dream than hers. I'd always thought a house should be *my* reward for sticking it out in the Bronx. For getting through life, doing what I needed to do, and not complaining about it like today's suburban housewives with their nannies, cooks, cleaning ladies, au pairs, and Mercedes, who talk endlessly about how hard they work and how tired they are. And if Mother had come with me to Bloomfield, we would have put the furniture where she wanted it put. The walls would have displayed the same tired, dusty prints that had been hanging in the foyer of our apartment for decades. The house would have been too cool in the winter and too warm in the summer, because those were the temperatures she preferred. And I'm sure she would have ended up in the master bedroom, because, after all, that's where the mother belongs.

She could have gotten us out of the Bronx years earlier, Nick, but instead she chose to hide her money from me. So why do I feel guilty? And why do I feel as if I'm being punished for my selfishness? It's as if God is saying, "Ah, Betty. I thought I'd tease you with an idyllic home for a few years, just so you could get used to having the life you always wanted. But it's time to pay the piper. Your mother says hello."

I realize I am going on a bit—and, looking over what I just wrote, I am wondering if I'll hit the "Send" button when I'm done typing here. You're probably not used to your Aunt Betty talking in such a manner, and frankly I'm not used to speaking in such a manner myself. But it's part of the crotchety old woman thing again. Life hardens you, Nick—you try to live a good life, you pay your taxes, you work 45 years, and nothing ever gets easier. When you're younger, you have the energy to roll with the punches and absorb most of what life throws at you, but as you continue to live, and you can't see as well, and you can't hear the way you used to, and you look in the mirror and see an old person looking back at you, you lose your ability to shrug off life and you start to rail against it. Which is what I suppose I've been doing in this e-mail.

So let me close with some advice. Do what you want to do while you still can. Don't have regrets, my dear Nicholas...live your life, take control of it. If you want that promotion at work and all the extra money that goes with it, make it happen. Rub elbows with the bigwigs. Tell them what they want to hear. Present the side of yourself that they want to see. In my years at the insurance company, I've watched it happen many times— smarmy agents and salespeople showing the honchos the better side of their faces and their secretaries the uglier side. Believe me, it works like a charm, and I wish I'd done more of it. Sometimes you have to tell people what they want to hear. That gives them the motivation they need to give you what you want.

Do call me, or write me, soon. If you do, I promise I won't say or do anything guilt-inducing. I've been following some of the cooking shows on PBS and would love to make you a home-cooked meal and hear about your life, your dreams, and (I hope) your latest lady love, who would be a fool to let you slip through her fingers.

Love,
Aunt Betty

Leo Lentricchia

(C)

October XX, 20XX
4271 ■■■■■■■■■■ Avenue
Throgs Neck, NY 10465

Transamerica Telephone
Personnel Dept.
1355 Broadway
NY, NY 10036

Dear Personnel Dept:

I am writing to apply for a job in your company. I am very interested in working at Transamerica Telephone as a lineman or
any other kind of starting job you have available, would also be
of interest to me.

I am a hardworking person who would work hard for your
company and put in many hours, as much time as you would
wish and on any day of the week. If you talk to my current
boss (Mr. Sam Pelosi, owner of Three Brothers delicatessen
in Throgs Neck NY) he will tell you that in four years I have
never missed one day of work, I even went to work on
Christmas eve and Easter so that people could have everything
they need for their family meals, and that meant I spent less
time with my own family, and I never complained. I also

worked when I was sick several times over the years so that Mr. Pelosi would not be left in the lerch. He always counts on me and trusts me completely, I open the deli on weekend mornings and two nights a week I close and take the money to the night deposit, there was never one penny missing in my four years at Three Brothers Deli. And even though I have a lot of friends none of them ever get free sandwiches from me because that is just not the way to run a business.

I am graduating from Bronx Community College with my AA degree in two months, so if college is important to you I will have that degree by the end of the year. My GPA is 2.7. I know it could be better but there is a reason. I have to work at least 30 hours a week at the deli (Mr. Pelosi counts on me for that) and sometimes as a result schoolwork has to suffer. Reading takes a lot of time and the deli is always busy so there is not a lot of time for reading textbooks and studying for tests which takes concentration. But think about it this way, When I work at the deli I am totally doing the job at all times and not thinking about reading books, writing papers, etc. And that is how I would be if I worked for your company. You would always have my full attention.

Hard work and honesty run in my family. Both of these things are very important to us. I learned all these skills from my father, who before he retired owned five supermarkets in the Bronx, and they were always the cleanest stores in bad areas where he could have made more money if he ripped off the poor people, but he never did and so everyone loved him. He was president of the Bronx Italian Society for a long time and people still talk about what a great man he is. And when it comes to work and honesty I know I follow in his footsteps. When you hire a man named Lentricchia you get the best man for the job. That is, a man who will make you proud and who will always be reliable and on time.

I know some people who work for your company and they always say it is a good company, there is a good union and the pay is good. Which are two things that I like but they are not the main reason for me wanting a job with you. I am studying communications and computers at Bronx CC, and the truth is I am very interested in communications especially cell phones and fiber optics. Everyone else thinks cell towers are ugly but I do not, I think they are amazing and if you would hire me, I would be glad to climb to the top of them and work on them. Even if it takes me several years to go up through the ranks to be able to do that, I will gladly wait my turn and learn everything I can, so that I can be valuable to your company. And meanwhile I would be doing something I find very interesting. In other words I think this would be perfect for both of us, because I would get to work in my chosen field and you would get a great worker who always wants to learn more, and is never lazy.

Although I live in Throgs Neck (section of Bronx) I will gladly work anywhere in New York City or anywhere else. It does not have to be convenient. For example, I have a car and so I could go to Staten Island for work. Or even far parts of Brooklyn or Long Island, or even New Jersey. So I am not tied into the subways and so you know I would never be late for work.

I think it is great that your company hires people and then helps them have careers. For example, my friend Roger Borelli who works for you, told me that his boss started on the line crew and now he's a manager with a car. I'm not saying I want a car or anything special, I am just saying that I think it is great that a company takes care of its people. It reminds me of my father who always gave benefits to the people who worked for him even though that meant less money in his pocket, it is just the right thing to do but a lot of companies don't do it, so that is another reason I would like a job with Transamerica Telephone.

Please call me at 917-■■■-6745 (Transamerica cell phone!) or you can email me at ■■■@transamerica.net (Transamerica Internet service!) and I will drop everything and come in for an interview.

Sincerely yours,
Leo A. Lentricchia

Leo A. Lentricchia
English 102
Mrs. Sylvia Weinstock
Bronx Community College

People Who Have Had an Influence on My Life*

When a person sits down to think about his life, he will have to ask himself several questions. Did he take care of people and treat them properly? Is his life something that made an impression on others? Was his influence good on other people or was it bad? When he gets married and has children will his kids look up to him? And will he make his parents as proud of him as he is of them? A person always wants to be a positive role model, so that he can have others think of him as someone who is valuable and worthy. And a good way to be a positive role model is to look at the people who have had an influence on your life, and then try to make sure you behave like them. More than that you should think like they think because when you think a certain way, you behave that way too. The people who are my biggest influences are all people who think and do. They are my father, my mother, and my friend Robert.

My father, Giovanni S. Lentricchia, is like the president of the country, except the country is his house and his business. He is a man who knows he has to rule the country so that the people do not get out of control. He always says, "If you give people an inch they will take a yard." So he is generous and he gives help

---

* Mrs W, I know we were supposed to write about only one person but I had a lot to say and I didn't think I could keep it to just one person. Sorry. –LAL

when people need it and deserve it, but he does not have patience for people who cannot help themselves and who are leaches on society. If you work hard and do not cheat or steal then you are a worthy person and there is nothing my father will not do for you. But if you try to cheat him or you are lazy then he casts you out, because you do not behave the right way. And if you come to the neighborhood to rob houses or make trouble, then you will learn very quickly that you do not belong there, and if you come back, you will learn other things too. At his work and in his house, everyone has to pull their share of the weight and respect the president, even if it means keeping quiet because you have to understand that the president makes the rules and sometimes you have to just live with them. My father influenced me, and taught me, that it is very easy to tell the difference between a good person and a bad person, and I use that information every day.

My mother, Concetta C. Lentricchia, is a huge influence on me and my family because she is a role model for girls and other women. My mother is a woman who understands how the world is. She is smart and she understands how things work. She believes that it is a woman's job to make the house clean and raise her kids to be good children who are going to be good mothers and fathers someday, too. For 25 years she worked for my father in his businesses, she never complained and he could not have done it without her, but at the same time the house was always clean and there was always great food, we never had a cook or a cleaning lady. She was an influence because she knows life is hard and she always makes the best of it, she is married to the "king" after all and she is his "queen" but there have been times when she was also his "slave" and again she never complained. My mother is all about hard work and love and that is why she is a role model, and a person with great influence. I know my two brothers and two sisters would say the same thing.

The third person who has influenced my life is my friend Robert Bornelli. We are friends for more than 15 years. We went to school together from the time we were kids. He is a popular guy and everyone likes him, and I know why that is true, he is helpful to people and he smiles and laughs and people like that. He was good at sports and that only made him more popular. He has a good job with the phone company where he got promoted twice because he is a hard worker. Robert is a person who has a lot of fun in life. Yes he works hard but not too hard, work isn't the only thing he thinks about. He still has a lot of friends from school, we all stay in touch and go out on weekends, and it is like old times when we were all on the baseball team together. He has not changed and that is a big influence on me. Some people change for the worse and then you don't like them any more, but Robert is still a good friend to me and he will be a good husband when he marries my sister Maria. Now he is not perfect, no one is, but he has been an influence on my life by showing me that life does not have to be all work, you can have both work and fun.

In conclusion, there are three people who have influenced my life and I was lucky to know all of them. And I know that they are powerful people because they influenced a lot of other people too. So they are role models for me.

Annette Bain

(D)

CONFIDENTIAL
To: Members of Tenure Committee for
    English Department Candidate Annette Bain
Fr: Gretel Liebtrau

The tenure packet compiled by Associate Professor Annette Bain is impressive. Having team-taught several courses with her, and having shared an office with her for the seven years she has been on faculty at Mendham College, I am pleased to serve on her tenure evaluation committee.

Dr. Bain's scholarly work is indeed impressive. I have read all the publications listed on her CV. The articles she's published in *Medieval Drama Quarterly*, *PMLA*, *Victorian Studies*, and *The Journal of Victoriana* point to her significant strengths in the area of contextual analysis and her intense, deep engagement with a specific slice of literary theory.

Her work is always passionate, never half-hearted. This quality can be seen in everything she has written, but it is especially evident in her controversial Fall 2004 contribution to *Insignificant Others: Woman as (Proto)Type in the Victorian Novel* (University of Chicago Press: M. Grenaux, ed.). Armed with an arsenal composed of decades of theoretical work in the Victorian novel, Dr. Bain advocated flamboyantly (and, some argued, perhaps a bit stridently) for the removal of Charles Dickens from the literary canon. Press coverage was unexpectedly wide, both in collegiate circles (*The Chronicle of Higher Education* profiled Dr. Bain in a full-page feature) and in the popular press. Articles in *The New York Times* and *The Christian Science Monitor* reporting on Dr. Bain's work generated the type of literary discussion rarely, if ever, seen in the news media. As a result, Dr. Bain was offered, and conducted, more than a dozen guest lectures at some of the nation's finest liberal arts colleges, including Smith, Sarah Lawrence, Amherst, Princeton, Columbia, Brown, and the University of Chicago. She was also invited to speak at several universities in Europe and Asia, where she received accolades. Most recently she has continued her aggressive de(con)struction of the canon of Victorian literature in *Fictional Art(i)(facts): Art and Narrative in the Victorian Novel(la)* (Norton, 2006). This complex, densely structured, difficult work can be read as Dr. Bain's critical and theoretical manifesto, and it too has been the subject of serious and intense debate.

The net effect of Dr. Bain's research and scholarly work has been the most decided enrichment of Mendham College, its faculty, and its student body. As a result of Dr. Bain's reputation, we have seen a marked increase in the number of young women coming to Mendham to major in English. Dr. Bain can also be credited with almost single-handedly reviving interest in upper-level courses that had not been offered in years and that had been canceled previously due to lack of enrollment. One of Dr. Bain's most popular courses, Critical Theory 414, never a favorite of Mendham English majors, is now offered every semester due to student demand. Another of Dr. Bain's courses, Medieval Drama 366, once taught every other spring, is now offered annually—again, as a result of significantly increased student demand.

Dr. Bain's prominence among our English faculty, achieved over such a short time period, has also helped the school of humanities attract young scholar/teachers in other disciplines. Daniel Barstow in the history department told me he accepted Mendham's offer as a result of his interview with Dr. Bain. Leila Chan in the fine arts department told Dean Althorp she turned down a faculty appointment at Carleton College for the same reason.

In her committee work Dr. Bain has been a steady, if not always enthusiastic, participant. She rarely misses a committee meeting, and her colleagues rely on her to execute her duties quickly and efficiently. I have not seen her go above and beyond the call of duty in these areas, perhaps because of the vigor with which she pursues the activities that are closer to her heart—advisor to the campus feminist newsletter, organizer of marches for social justice on City Hall, vice-chair of the committee for curriculum reform. In all these endeavors, she leads by example and embodies the ideals of the liberal arts and higher education.

At the department level, Dr. Bain is highly respected but considered by some to be divisive. She attends all department meetings, but I have occasionally seen her turn the agenda from workaday topics to matters that seem to be more of personal import than departmental business. Here, as in all other areas of her academic career, Dr. Bain advocates passionately for the changes in which she believes. For example, she has been instrumental in bringing to fruition the English department's Get Ahead initiative, in which local companies fund scholarships for women of all backgrounds to study the liberal arts at Mendham College.

A reading of Dr. Bain's student evaluations over the last ten semesters offers a wide range of opinion. For every devoted fan, Dr. Bain has an equally vociferous detractor. In general, Dr. Bain receives high evaluations for her upper-level majors courses and significantly lower evaluations for her freshman writing courses. It is impossible to garner the gender distribution due to the blind nature of evaluations, but a close reading indicates the probability that Dr. Bain's following is primarily among women. There does seem to be a disturbing current through the 101 evaluations: Many students, particularly those who appear to be male and on sports teams, comment negatively on what they see as Dr. Bain's dismissive treatment of them. However, as we all know, student evaluations are highly subjective and may be based on personal animosity, deservedly low grades, or any number of other factors that may or may not reflect teacher performance.

The above are the objective criteria on which the tenure committee must base its decision. Yet we must certainly acknowledge that there is always a degree to which subjectivity plays a role in each committee member's vote in favor of or against tenure. I must therefore acknowledge the subjective areas that have influenced my final vote.

As a tenured faculty member of Mendham's English department, and a twenty-year teacher of literature at this fine institution, I have always operated on the assumption that the ideal faculty member is one who combines active research with care and concern for our student population. As our student body grows more diverse and we attract more first-generation students, it becomes all the more important that our work tip toward teaching and student support. So many of our students find the liberal arts increasingly irrelevant, and it is our obligation, and our joy, to correct this misperception. To be effective in that role, we must walk alongside our students, not stand over them. While it has always been difficult to balance the demands of scholarly work with our students' significant needs, the best faculty members achieve that balance with panache. They do so because they believe in both sides of their job equally, sometimes favoring one side, sometimes the other, while managing to achieve an equilibrium over the course of their careers.

And it is in that word "career" that I see the most difficulty with granting tenure to the candidate. From her scholarship through her publications, from her work on campus to her work with students, Dr. Bain has always seemed to me to put her academic "career" first and foremost. Her published work does not evince a love of scholarship, but rather a desire to tear down idols in an effort to increase her own reputation—as well as her desirability on the academic job market. To be effective educators, we must not see our students as stepping stones to something bigger and better, and yet I fear this is precisely Dr. Bain's approach to even her brightest students.

Tenure can offer the greatest of academic freedom, and it is the gift that all devoted faculty work toward and hope for. In my (admittedly traditional) style of thinking, an offer of tenure is the offer of a contract between a teacher/scholar and the institution: The institution offers a hospitable environment for research and study, and the tenured professor offers a tacit guarantee that s/he wishes to remain at that institution for the length of her career. The situation is intended to be mutually beneficial.

And yet I do not believe that Dr. Bain would remain at Mendham College for the remainder of her career. She clearly desires a more high-profile appointment at a larger, more exclusive institution, and I can only imagine that such an offer will not be long in coming, given her devotion to journal publishing and convention attendance. Dr. Bain will leave us at the drop of a hat, but she is looking for the security of tenure, and the higher salary of a full professor, in the meantime. This is not a reason to accept tenure, and it is certainly enough of a reason for the committee not to offer it.

It is my recommendation that Dr. Annette Bain be denied tenure.

Gretel Liebtrau
Professor of English

Tomás Rodriguez
(E)

From the private journal of Tomás Rodriguez

No awful dreams last night—thank you, Lord. Is this your way of telling me I've made the right decision? What you put me through for the last two weeks—was it a way of testing my mettle or my resolve?

How ironic that a man who helps others analyze their dreams can't extract meaning, or answers, from his own. I think I see, though, the punishment in my attempts to flee from them, to shut them down or at least not remember them. The first three nights after I sent the letter were nights of torture— lying in the abyss between consciousness and unconsciousness— my mind racing from one image to the next, like a race car going ever faster and threatening to spin out of control at any minute, yet each time the crash was imminent, and blessed consciousness about to return—the speeding automobile found another path, another track around which to careen, and on and on until the alarm finally woke me to start another day, exhausted before it had even begun.

And you know how the days are—I must have the energy I need and that the world needs from me. The people are so needy—no, they are not needy—they have hurts and pain, and I must help absorb their cares and remain strong, while my own reserves are depleted through lack of nourishment and lack of sleep. Declan tells me he is worried about me, about my appetite, about my weight loss in the last few months—and it is true that my appetite, never strong, has been nonexistent for the last two weeks. Yesterday a child on the playground offered me a grape, making sure to choose the largest one from the small cluster in her Ziploc bag, and no sooner had my teeth broken the skin than my stomach lurched and my throat shut, refusing to allow sustenance into my sinful body. The child watched me expectantly, awaiting a smile to confirm the sweetness of the offering and the pleasure of sharing—and I could not disappoint her—so I hid the grape in my cheek and pretended to swallow—and ran into the lavatory to spit it into the toilet before sinking to my knees as my stomach contracted and my esophagus became acidic—as my body tried to expel the contents to which it had refused access.

And for the days to be so long and draining, and then the nights to offer no rest, I began to fear for—not myself—but those others who count on me, who rely on me, who need me to help them through *their* days and nights, whose problems are so much greater than my own. The mother who lost her oldest son in Desert Storm, and her youngest son in Iraq.—The teenage girls whose divorced parents bring home different bed partners, modeling the behavior that leads their daughters to a never-ending cycle of pregnancy, abortion, poverty, and abuse.—The older women who've cared for their children and whose husbands have divorced them or died, trying to find meaning and purpose while struggling to keep a roof over their heads. And the boys, too—abandoned by their fathers, courted by gangs, hiding the hurt, trying to suck it up and take it like a man.—And the middle-aged men, losing their hair, exhausted from working long hours to pay mortgages on overpriced houses they can't afford, tempted by the simplicity of an affair, a desire to feel young again, a nostalgia for a past where they played baseball, cruised the streets in their convertibles, and had sex with girls they never planned to marry.

And so yes, after three nights of this torture and with a body ready to revert to dust, I pulled out the chest from under my bed. I had to go into the yard at midnight to retrieve the key I buried under the wisteria bush in my efforts to prevent myself from accessing the chest's contents. I know I was not thinking clearly—the dreams had turned into hallucinations in which aborted babies and crucified criminals paced back and forth in my room, howling and crying and staring at me with their bloodshot eyes. I had to escape them—and your test—and so I took three of the pills to escape consciousness and the golems of the shadowy netherworld just beyond the waking state.

But the bliss of a mind made blank through three sharp-edged little pills, always so reliable in the past, was not to be achieved. For the visions and specters became even more insistent and demanding, HIS shape and sound never in the center but always off to the side, the one minute smiling, happy, coaching his soccer team, laughing with the children and their parents—the next minute brutally fucking, yes *fucking*, a prostitute, pummeling her face with his fists as his cock pounds into her—then emerging from the East River, water dripping from his musculature, with the unconscious, almost-drowned boy (named Tommy in the vision, the name never spoken but *known* by the mind) clinging to him—then sitting quietly in the church tower with a high-powered rifle, its sights aimed on me and Declan, and my looking up to see him there, and our eyes meet and we communicate without words: *I know what you are doing, and I'm going to stop you.* But has he said that to me, or have I said that to him?

And finally I understood—as only a waking man on the verge of collapse can understand—that you were once again telling me I cannot go around this process, I must go through it, no shortcuts and no easy pathways. The deed is done—the letter has been sent—there is no changing anything now. Except—I can warn him. I can tell him what I've done. With proper warning, he can take care of himself, especially if he knows to watch for what is coming. But I fear for my own life. I know what he's done to others—what would he to do me, without hesitation? I know, I know, after these two long weeks, that my existence is more valuable than his—I touch more people, do more good. If it comes down to one of us, I am the one who must survive.

And what happens when the assassin succeeds in dispatching Joseph Castro? The world is rid of a great force of evil, a devil masquerading in the shoes of a concerned citizen, the worst form of hypocrite—a man who will not only hire murderers but actively solicit murder, as a topic to be studied, a phenomenon to be observed and reported upon. A sociopath, a psychopath—the clinical terms are unnecessary. The proper term is *evil*, pure and simple.

I did not ask, Lord, to fight evil. All I ever wanted was to do good. But you have chosen me to help eliminate evil from the world, and now I know I must accept your work without question, though it has been hard, so hard to make these decisions knowing the cost to my soul. You did not have to help me, but you did, yesterday—and I thank you. There is no such thing as coincidence—You needed me to see him after coaching the girls' soccer team, his eyes and hands lingering too long on the arm of young, innocent Lindsay Moran, in age a girl but in body a blossoming woman. I understood, in the blink of an eye, that he would violate that girl, perhaps already had done so. And then what is Lindsay's future—to be wife number three, beaten and abused before being cast out?

A tidal wave washed over me—and when the water receded my peace was restored. I slept last night, the sleep of angels and dead babies. Because I knew, finally, that the visions, the horrors, of the past two weeks were not visited upon me by you—but rather by your dark rival to tempt me—and make me doubt you—and weaken my resolve to do the work you have given me.

My small appetite returned this morning—I had a slice of toast for breakfast and two slices of bologna for lunch. Declan did not comment but nodded approvingly, and smiled. I long to confide in him but I know I must not.

So now I sit and wait, wondering if I will be asked to deliver the eulogy.

A

The Carrie Morrison Literary Agency
386 West ■■th Street, New York, NY 10025

Joan Ventre
Senior Editor
Manor House Publishers
40 E. ■■th Street
New York, NY 10010

Dear Joan:

Here's the proposal for *The Everyday Killer*, which we talked about earlier today. As I mentioned, the author is in the process of completing the research on the book. He expects to complete the manuscript in about six months.

With all the ho-hum projects we see in a world where everyone wants his or her name on a book jacket, it's exceedingly rare to find a book proposal that makes my jaw drop open. *The Everyday Killer* is that book. It's the natural evolution of everything we're seeing in the mass media, the next step beyond *CSI* and *48 Hours* and *20/20* special reports on unsolved murders. Today's books, TV shows, and movies reassure the reader/viewer that *murder is something that happens to someone else*. It happens to bad people like drug dealers, in bad places like the ghetto and the underworld of organized crime. It's a comforting illusion to the middle and upper classes, but the statistics show the truth of the matter: Most murders are committed by someone known to the victim, for reasons that usually revolve around petty jealousies, envy, and misunderstandings. *The Everyday Killer* warns the reader, in no uncertain terms, that *someone may be plotting your murder even as you read the book*.

I'd like to see Stephen King or James Patterson create a more suspenseful premise.

The author—I'll call him "A" for now, as he requires anonymity, for obvious reasons—is a decent writer with a good sense of narrative structure and pacing. I think his proposed table of contents is perfect, though I think the title could be sexier. We'll work on that, of course. I don't expect any problems with A's making the manuscript delivery schedule. Getting the book from him is my top priority, which means that as soon as I have it, you will, too.

Joan, I don't want to pressure you, but I've had a lot of interest, and I'm not going to be able to keep the lid on this one too much longer. If we can agree to terms within a week, I won't put it up for auction. If we can't, then an auction is the only way to guarantee that A gets what he deserves for what is sure to be a massive best-seller, with serious TV/film crossover potential.

Give me a call on my cell any time. I'm around.

Best,
Carrie

Book Proposal
The Everyday Killer

Alternates:
The Mind of a Murderer
The Mind of a Killer
Common Homicide
Circle of Assassins

What drives someone to murder?

Mystery novelists are fond of creating intricate plots in which murders are carefully plotted and executed. Clues are left behind for the sleuth to find and analyze. Suspects are identified and questioned. Just when the investigator is about to give up, he has a hunch. Revisiting a specific suspect and probing deeper—or looking at the crime from a different perspective—the detective has an epiphany. The murderer is caught or brought to some type of justice, whether legal, vigilante, or poetic.

In real life, however, most murders aren't quite so intricate. A jealous boyfriend stalks and kills his ex-girlfriend. A beaten-once-too-often wife drugs her husband, ties him to the bed, pours gasoline on him, and sets him on fire. Two gangs tussle over turf, and kids die in the process. A drug dealer tries to skim a little off the top and finds himself in a Staten Island landfill. Two drunken guys in the parking lot of a football stadium argue over who has the right of way; one pulls out a gun and shoots the other one through the head. This is the non-plot-driven, workaday manner in which murder happens in the world around us.

But sometimes fiction and nonfiction merge. In the real world, people *do* sometimes scheme, and connive, and plot to kill someone—a former friend, current lover, estranged business partner, or political rival. Maybe the would-be murderer is an older woman who's fed up with the drug dealer who's terrorizing her neighborhood. Maybe it's a brother with incestuous fantasies plotting against his sister's fiancé. Maybe an underappreciated college professor seeks revenge on an administrator whose views of education don't match hers. And maybe a bereaved parent, failed by the criminal justice system, wants to take the pedophile who murdered her child off the streets permanently.

The Everyday Killer answers the question that no amount of Court TV coverage, and no true-crime saga, has ever answered in a satisfactory manner: *What drives everyday people to murder?* In *The Everyday Killer* I will present five case studies (all 100% non-fiction, with identities and place names disguised, of course) of desperate people—our friends and neighbors, our brothers and sisters—who decided to take the law into their own hands. These are not high-profile cases; they all took place in a major metropolitan area in the last two decades, and the killers were never found. *The Everyday Killer* solves each crime, taking the reader step by step through each facet of the murder plot, introducing the murderers before their victims, carrying the reader along on a horrifying journey of anger, betrayal, and vengeance.

I am well qualified to write *The Everyday Killer*, having studied the criminal mind for more than a decade, and having worked with hardened, remorseless criminals for whom murder is child's play. No one who has read *The Everyday Killer* will go to sleep with their doors and windows unlocked ever again. The book will destroy the innocence and naïveté of the typical American, who foolishly imagines that no one wishes him or her harm. For, as *The Everyday Killer* shows, someone may be plotting your death at this very moment.

Part 3

Freddy d'Arget

If you nosed around Freddy d'Arget's house, you'd notice certain items missing, things found in every other home in Bloomfield, New Jersey.

There were no clocks, because Freddy never had to be anywhere by a specific time. There were no dishes and no glassware at 145 ■■■■ ■■■■■■■ Road, either. A few days after Freddy moved in, a group of friends had stopped by to celebrate his return. They'd ordered pizza and take-out Chinese, and they'd used the delicate china his parents had received as a wedding gift. Then someone (probably Rock, who was always the first to start these kinds of things) announced that he was Greek, and that Greeks like to smash plates to express approval for the meal they've just consumed. So everyone had begun smashing the plates against the walls (stains from the marinara sauce still showed against the white paint), onto the hardwood floor (in which bits of dried cheese were now permanently embedded), and into the fireplace (where shards remained). Later that evening, someone else had the idea of using the tumblers (which his mother had collected from boxes of dishwashing detergent decades earlier, and which would have brought nice sums on eBay) for target practice in the backyard. The person who smashed the most glasses got to take two hits on the bong for every one hit taken by everyone else. Freddy had won that contest.

The kitchen also lacked food in the pantry and cleaning products in the cabinets. Thanks to Pizza Hut, KFC, and Burger King, there was no need to keep food in the house. As for cleaning, Freddy wasn't ready to relive the first twenty-two years of his life, which he'd spent trying to escape from the smell of the ammonia and bleach with which his mother had scrubbed everything in her path.

He knew his mother's obsession with cleanliness was one of the reasons his father had left. You couldn't go anywhere or do anything in the house without Ma after you to clean up your mess. As soon as you walked in the front door, she was down on her knees with a wet rag, frantically trying to keep the tile floor pristine. Dad couldn't watch a football game or read the paper without that fucking vacuum cleaner creating a black hole into which everything, including the TV's unreliable reception, got sucked. To keep his mother happy, or at least to shut her up, his father had beaten him black and blue when he tracked mud into the house or made a mess in the basement.

She was a tough woman to live with, his mother. All she cared about was *what people would say*. What would the neighbors say if they knew her husband moonlighted as a truck driver? What would her sister's family say if they didn't give her nephew a generous enough gift for his wedding? What would the people at the bank say when she began drawing on the family's savings, due to her husband's inability to find and hold down a job?

Yup, that was Ma for you. Everything was a reflection on *her*. What you wore to church spoke to her ability to dress you properly. The way you spoke, the friends you made, were a comment on her ability to mold your character and choose your associates. How you behaved in school was the direct result of what she'd done right (everything) or wrong (nothing).

Was it any wonder that all of Ma's kids had ended up messed up or dead? Of the three of them, only Freddy was left. Claudia had been sent away at age fifteen, when she'd "gotten in trouble." Freddy still remembered the scene, with Ma slapping Claudia's face and screaming she wouldn't let people say she'd raised a slut. Off Claudia had gone to live with relatives in

Maryland, and he'd never seen her again. She'd died of a drug overdose on a Fourth of July weekend when she was eighteen. Freddy couldn't remember going to her funeral service. And Ma certainly couldn't have gone either, because Freddy couldn't remember his mother ever leaving Bloomfield.

Zack managed to survive a little longer. He'd gotten unruly when Dad left. He'd always been his father's favorite, and he couldn't figure out whom he hated most: Dad for leaving, Mom for making him go, or himself for not being able to stop it. He took out his anger on anyone in his path: teachers, friends, kids on the block, his brother, his sister. When he stopped punching walls and started punching people, Ma got afraid. And when he finally punched Ma—square in the mouth, knocking out two of her teeth—she couldn't ignore the situation any longer. Off he went to military school, never to return home. He eventually entered the Navy and died after being stabbed at a brothel in Shanghai.

After Claudia and Zack left, it was just him and Ma for a while. They stayed out of each other's way. Ma worked full time at the bank ("to pay the mortgage that your no-good father left me holding," she'd say, daily), so he didn't see much of her. That left him plenty of time to hang with his friends, who were making daily trips into New York City to cop dime bags of pot. Getting stoned kept him mellow and stopped him from knocking the rest of Ma's teeth out.

When he was twenty-two and bartending at an extremely tough place on Route 46 frequented by bikers, he met Lorna. He'd stay with her for days, getting high, eating, and sleeping, then repeating the cycle. When he returned home to get a change of clothes Ma would barely have noticed that he'd been gone.

Lorna wanted to go to California. L.A., she said, or San Diego, where perpetual summer reigned and where they could surf and live on the beach. When Freddy announced he'd be moving to California, Ma simply said, "I hear it's beautiful."

When he moved back into the house after she died, he found her diary, which she'd kept sporadically over the years. He looked up the entry for the day he'd left for Los Angeles:

> *F. left for California today. Thank God he's gone–the last of my burdens. Now I can have some peace and quiet, and the house all to myself. I just hope him and his whore girlfriend stay away for good.*

The purpose of moving to California was to have a good time, not to work like a slave for some asshole business owner. But he and Lorna needed money. The choice was obvious: sell some pot here, some mescaline there. He always dealt fairly. His "clients" got their shit when they wanted it, and he never adulterated the stuff to stretch it farther. He and Lorna made a fair profit that paid the rent on an oceanside shanty in Redondo Beach.

He should have kept to the light stuff, but then heroin and cocaine started getting big, and there was a lot of money to be made. But the money they made somehow disappeared into their veins and up their noses. Still, there were plenty of good times, always lots of friends around. Until the night Lorna snorted a particularly long and thick line, opened her eyes wide, grabbed her chest, gagged, and keeled over dead.

For a few weeks he tried to clean up his act—get a job—go straight—but nobody would hire him. So he went back to dealing heroin and doing plenty of it himself. One Sunday afternoon he went to pick up a large shipment from his usual contact. The usual contact wasn't there, but another man was. Billy said he was "taking over." It turned out that Billy was a member of the narcotics squad, and Freddy landed in jail for eight years.

He tried calling his mother to ask her to send him the money to pay for a decent lawyer instead of the public defender. When she didn't answer the phone, he left a message for her with one of the neighbors. She didn't call back. He wrote to her from jail twice and never received a response. When he'd served his time and been set free he tried to call her again—the first time in eight years—and found that the phone number he'd grown up with had been changed. The new number was unlisted.

He'd been out of prison, living in a halfway house and half-heartedly looking for a job, when news of his mother's death arrived. He was the sole heir. The house in New Jersey, plus about fifty thousand dollars in savings, was all his.

He was both overjoyed and shocked. Overjoyed that he'd have a comfortable place to live and money to spend. Shocked that Ma had left him everything. But Ma was too selfish to give her money to charity or to strangers, so Freddy ended up with everything by default.

He used some of Ma's money to see if he could track down Dad. He'd thought a lot about his father when he was in jail, and he wanted to see the old man just one more time and ask him three questions: *Why did you do it? Why did you leave us without saying good-bye? How could you be there on Tuesday and gone on Wednesday?*

But Mr. d'Arget was long dead, taken by a heart attack while watching the Super Bowl in his comfortable two-bedroom retirement house in Tucson, which he shared with his lady friend, Maude.

"There must be a mistake," Maude said, genuinely surprised. "Al didn't have any kids."

Freddy had the best of intentions. He'd move into the house, settle in, and then find a job. He'd learned carpentry in the prison's trade program, and he was pretty good at it. But first there were some old friends he wanted to look up.

The old Jersey gang, who'd visited him in California before he got arrested and thrown in jail, was happy to have him back. Their ranks had thinned over the years, but everyone who was still alive hadn't changed: wild and crazy Rock, daring Earl, philosophical Henry, literary Will. Most of them were still living in the same places they'd been living for years, usually their parents' basements or attics. None of them were married, none of them had kids, and they all dealt.

So many goodies had come onto the streets during Freddy's years in prison. The club kids were wild for X, K, and crystal meth, and the black market for Viagra was going strong. Just to be with his old friends, he helped out with a few deals, did some courier work.

The X, especially, helped him forget the past and made him feel content. The house held so many memories, all bad. The scent from Ma's ammonia lingered in every room, and Dad's shadow lurked in every corner. He nailed the door to Claudia's old bedroom shut so he wouldn't be reminded of her. Not that any trace of Claudia had remained, anyway. His mother had made sure of that when she'd converted Claudia's pink-and-yellow oasis into a sterile sewing room.

And the neighbors on ■■■■ ■■■■■■■ Road were even worse now than they'd been when he was growing up. Still nosy, still minding everyone's business but their own, still watching and gossiping. They'd taken one look at him and hated him instantly. No one made him feel welcome; parents brought their kids inside when he sat on his front steps drinking a few beers.

So what if he liked to have fun? And so what if he didn't work? They were all jealous of him, jealous that he owned a house, had money, and didn't have to do the nine-to-five grind like they did, just to pay a mortgage on some shitty Cape Cod on a 50' x 100' lot. Well, he didn't give a shit. He could make more money in one week, just by sitting in his own house and letting everyone else come to him, than the petty assholes on ■■■■ ■■■■■■■ Road could make in a month.

And they did come to him, all night long, three or four nights a week. Kids from the suburbs no longer had to go to

New York, Newark, Paterson, or Passaic to get what they needed. They just pulled into the driveway of Freddy's modest, once well-kept home, knocked on the back door, and left five minutes later with enough X and crystal meth to last them the weekend.

As word of his convenient location and ready supply spread, his client base rapidly expanded. After his arrests (which didn't stick for various reasons, including illegal searches and well-meaning judges who thought he deserved another chance) he'd gotten more careful. For those who understood the code, his answering machine message provided all the relevant information. Each week a different knock served as the signal, and each week buyers needed to use that special knock on a different door. On Wednesday he'd set his schedule for the week, then answer the door only during the appointed hours, not a minute earlier or a minute later. It was the only way to protect himself. No way was he going back to jail.

He expected the upcoming four-day holiday weekend to be a busy one. He was fully stocked up and expected to make at least two or three grand.

After that, who knew? It was hard to turn down easy money, but he'd liked the carpentry work he'd learned during his time inside, and he thought he might like to put those skills to work. It would suck to work for some asshole owner of a construction company, though. Especially when he could make a lot more money, and get a lot less aggravated, by just sitting home.

Well, whatever. He'd explore his options next week. There was no rush.

Roger Borelli

Roger liked to think of himself as an easygoing guy. A lover, not a fighter. Give him a few beers with his friends, dinner at a nice restaurant with his fiancée, and vacations in Atlantic City or Las Vegas, and he was happy. Life was too short not to enjoy it, right? When you worked 40, 45, 50 hours a week (including overtime, for which you got paid double time and a half, thanks to the union), you needed to have as much fun as you could.

He'd had this philosophy as a kid, then as a teenager, and now as an adult. In grammar school, he'd done just enough work to get promoted each year. His indulgent mother used to joke that he was a "solid C student." He could have done a lot better if he'd worked harder, applied himself, spent more time in front of the books and less time hanging out in the basement with his friends, but it was hard to get mad at Roger. While lamenting his average performance in math, science, or social studies, his teachers made a point of telling Rog's folks how much they liked him and enjoyed having him in class. His classmates felt the same way. Rog's easygoing attitude, sense of humor, and lack of drive and ambition made him popular across the various high school subcultures. He himself fell into the jock category (pitcher on the baseball team, occasional member of the swim team, big-time supporter of the football and basketball teams), but he also managed to remain on friendly terms with the burnouts, punks, stoners, and brains.

Roger had two brothers and a sister, all of whom gave Mr. and Mrs. Borelli much cause for concern in one way or another. But they never worried about Roger. *People like him*, they said.

He's good looking, funny, and popular. He'll always have a job and make money. He's got plenty of girls interested in him. He's all set.

He'd been lucky enough to get the job with the phone company almost as soon as he graduated high school. One of his buds had a brother who worked there, and the brother (who was a fan of Rog's, like everyone else) talked to the right people and got Rog hired. True to form, Rog had slipped into life at the phone company with ease. Within a week he was going to sports bars with the guys from his crew and renting summer bungalows with them at the Jersey shore.

And wasn't that what life should be about, after all? Working to make money, putting a little bit away (he and Maria were saving to buy a house, though her folks had so much money they could have given her one), and spending the rest on food, drink, concerts, sporting events, and vacations.

Stepping out of the shower, Rog found himself feeling gloomy, a rare state of mind for him. He much preferred to be happy. But he had to face facts. A dark cloud had descended on his life as soon as he and Maria had announced their engagement. He'd pushed it back as long as he could, thinking that ignoring the problem would make it go away. But it seemed to be getting worse.

This should have been the happiest time of his life, and it was turning out to be anything but. Maria wasn't the problem, of course. Rog hadn't been in any rush to settle down. Women flirted with him everywhere he went, and he could have had his pick. But Maria was exceptional. She understood him. She took care of him. She respected him. She didn't smother him. She didn't mind when he went to football games, Atlantic City, or casinos on Indian reservations with his buddies from high school and work. In fact, she encouraged it, saying that there was a time for testosterone and a time for estrogen, and that she'd get her fix of estrogen while he was out with his friends.

They also shared an Italian heritage. His family was from Naples, hers from Bari. His family was more Americanized, hers more traditional, so they couldn't live together before the wedding, but he knew they'd have no trouble when they moved in together. Maria was a traditional girl, accustomed to and comfortable with traditional roles, which was just what he needed. His mother had cooked for him, cleaned his room, and washed his clothes, and he wanted a wife who'd do the same. And while Maria had gone to community college and held a job on the customer service hotline of a soft-drink company, everyone knew that once she got married, her home would become her priority and kids would quickly follow.

You don't just marry a girl, you marry a family, Rog's friend Dylan had said to him just a few days ago, after the most recent incident. *Don't do what I did and marry the wrong family.*

Roger remained in a funk as he shaved and got dressed. He and Maria were meeting another couple for dinner and drinks at a trendy new restaurant in the City whose claims to fame were its $175 *prix fixe* dinner and its three-month waiting list. Maria had made the reservation way back when, and they'd all been looking forward to it. It was an excuse to go out for a night on the town, order expensive wine, then walk around the Village and buy things from the street vendors.

But tonight he was having a hard time feeling enthusiastic. He hadn't told Maria about the most recent incident, not wanting to make a big deal of it, not wanting to upset her. But he was starting to resent the way she was handling, or not handling, the problem. She did a lot of crying, and some begging and pleading, but he was still caught in the middle. It was her job, not his, to take a stand with her family. All she had to do was say *I'm putting my foot down, Leo. You're going to end this nonsense once and for all, or else.* But she wasn't putting her foot down, and his attempts to ignore the problem weren't making it go away. If anything, they seemed to be making it worse.

His mood didn't improve as he laced up his shoes. *There's no good time to have this conversation,* he thought. *But if I don't get it off my chest, I'm going to be in a foul mood all night. She's not going to want to talk about it, as usual. She's going to complain that I'm ruining her big night in the City. But we're going to talk about it tonight, and if she doesn't do something about it–soon–the wedding is off.*

There was light rap on the door, and Maria walked in. She was wearing a new dress and new shoes. Sparkle gel in her expensively dyed blonde tresses caught the light. Roger noticed, too, that she was carrying the Coach bag her mother had recently bought for her, which had set the old *strega* back $900. He couldn't have cared less about brand names, but Maria (and her mother and sister) seemed inordinately attached to them. Her father was that way, too. He always referred to his "Cadillac," never to his "car." Roger and his working-class parents simply couldn't keep up with the procession of brand names. On more than one occasion over the last few months, he'd wanted to say to Mr. and Mrs. Lentricchia *At least my folks don't have any violent fucked-up kids*, but he'd kept his mouth shut out of respect to Maria, and also because it wasn't quite true.

"Hey," Maria said, putting her purse down on the couch. Looking Roger up and down, she saw that he was wearing the overpriced, black-patterned Lucky Brand shirt she'd bought for him a few weeks earlier. "That shirt looks good on you."

"Thanks," Rog murmured, not quite making eye contact.

Maria immediately sensed a problem. When Rog didn't greet her with a smile, or a hug, or a kiss—or all three—he was pissed off about something.

Her back went up slightly. He wasn't going to have an attitude tonight of all nights, was he, when they'd be spending $350 for dinner, plus drinks, tip, and parking?

"What's wrong?" she asked, bluntly, impatiently.

"Listen, I have to get this off my chest, OK? You know how I am. Once I say it, I'll be fine."

"All right. What's up?"

"Your brother."

Maria drew in a breath and went on the defensive. "Rog, I don't want to have this conversation again. We've been over it a thousand times. I don't know what more you want me to do."

This was exactly the response Rog had expected. He threw down the gauntlet.

"I'll tell you right now, you're gonna do *something*. I've had it up to here with your family's bullshit. *Especially* your brother's."

"What's the problem now? You haven't seen each other in a month."

"The *problem*, in case you don't remember, is that he tried to kill me."

Maria took another deep breath and spoke slowly. "Look, Rog. Everyone knows you two have had some problems. I just don't understand why you both can't go your separate ways and stay out of each other's hair."

"I'll tell you why. Because he did it again today."

"Did what?"

"Snuck up behind me and sucker punched me."

"What! Where?"

"At the diner. I'm walking back to the truck, minding my own business, and bang—I get punched in the back. I was carrying coffee and it fucking scalded me."

"Jesus, Rog. What did you do?"

"What do you think I did? I threw the coffee in his face, then I beat the living fuck out of him. This time there wasn't anyone around to save his ass. I left him laying in the parking lot."

Maria broke down. "My God. My God. What's *wrong* with the two of you? Why do you hate each other so much?"

"Why do *I* hate *him*? The question is, Why does *he* hate

me? I never did anything to him. Nothing. Zero. Never stole one of his girlfriends, never robbed his car, never even looked at him the wrong way. I didn't even know he fucking *existed* until I met you."

"What are you talking about? You two were in the same home room every year of high school!"

"Yeah, OK. He hung around with his loser friends smoking pot under the bleachers. So forgive me for not wanting to be part of his fucking loser posse."

"And maybe that attitude showed through."

"Why does any of this matter *now*? High school was ten years ago. There's plenty of people I didn't really know back then, it doesn't mean they have it in for me *now*. When me and you started going out, I tried talking to him and inviting him to games. He just gave me the cold shoulder. So fuck him. I tried. And I'm sick of trying."

"Right. So instead of trying, you decide to throw hot coffee in his face."

"Are you listening to one word I'm saying? I was minding my own business, *again*, and he attacked me *for no reason*. All I was doing was stopping at a diner to pick up lunch. I can't wait to hear what his excuse is this time. Maybe he thought I was going in to fuck one of the waitresses."

"You weren't, were you?"

Roger, who'd been pacing back and forth, stopped dead in his tracks. "What?"

"I said, you weren't, were you?"

"What the fuck is that supposed to mean?"

"I asked you a question. You mind answering it?"

"OK, Marie. Yeah. Yeah, I was going into the diner to fuck every waitress there. I'm fucking each and every one of them in my free time."

"A simple 'No' would have been fine."

"Now you think I cheat on you? Your brother talks insane bullshit into your ears and you fucking *believe* him?"

"Calm down, Rog, OK? All I know is you *do* go to T&A bars. And you *do* go to bachelor parties. You think I live under a rock? I know what goes on at those things."

"I don't believe this. You always say you don't care if I have fun with my friends. That you trust me."

"I do trust you. But Jesus Christ, you're gonna be thirty years old, and you're getting married in a year. Don't you think it's time to grow up and stop going to sleazebag places to check out tits? *That's* my brother's problem with you, and you know it. He thinks it's disrespectful to me, and you know what? He's right. He tells my father, and my father tells my mother. So how much respect are they supposed to have for you when you're a grown man who still acts like a teenager?"

"You never said this before."

"I shouldn't have to. Maybe if you thought about *my* feelings, instead of just thinking about *your* good times with *your* buddies, you would have figured it out on your own."

"Come on, Marie. We know all the owners and the other guys. They're just hangouts. So what if there are some topless girls? You see tits everywhere, not just in bars."

"And do you slide money into girls' G-strings everywhere, too?"

"It's just what guys do."

"That's your excuse for everything. 'It's what guys do.' Any time you do something irresponsible or selfish, it's 'what guys do.' Now look. I'm not justifying what my brother's been doing. But I'm not gonna tell you I think he's totally out of line either, because he isn't. Leo's my big brother, and he's just like my father. They want to see the women in their lives treated with respect, and your behavior isn't respectful. Not to me, and not to my sister or mother either."

"How did your mother and sister get into this?"

"My mother invites you for Sunday dinner, and you say no because you'd rather go to a football game. How's that supposed to make her feel? She's trying to bring you into the family, even cooks the food you like, and you diss her so you can get drunk at a Giants game. Same thing with my sister. Her and her husband invite us over for dinner, and you do everything you can to get out of it. So what are they supposed to think?"

"He's fucking boring."

"No, he isn't. He's funny and smart. But he's not one of your group so you won't even give him the time of day. He told Connie he doesn't even want to be in the wedding party because you guys freeze him out."

"So let him drop out then."

Maria narrowed her eyes. "When you say things like that, *I* want to punch your face."

Roger suddenly felt like a cad. "All right, listen. I'm sorry. I'm really worked up about this. I don't want it to get worse. I'll try harder. I will. I promise. But you have to put your foot down. Everyone in your family's afraid of your father. Talk to him, get him to set Leo's ass straight, instead of trying to work it out with Leo on your own or having your mother run interference. It's the only way. Because I'm telling you, if he doesn't cut the shit, I'm gonna end up killing him. And you know I can. I'm much bigger and a lot stronger than he is."

"Great, Rog. I come here so we can go out for a nice dinner with our friends, and you tell me you're planning to kill my brother."

"Stop talking stupid, all right? I'm not *planning* anything. I'm saying that if he attacks me, I'm gonna fight back. I'm not gonna start anything with him, but I'm not gonna be some fucking pussy whose brother-in-law stalks him and thinks he can get away with it. And now you know it the same way he does."

"I know it the same way he does? What does *that* mean?"

"It means that when he was laying in the parking lot, I told him what I just told you. Basically, 'Stay the fuck away from me or I'll kill you.'"

"And what did he say, or did you knock him unconscious?"

"Oh, the motherfucker responded all right. Something like, 'Yeah, the joke's on you, asshole. You'll be dead first.'"

Maria didn't say a word. Rog continued slowly, seriously. "You didn't hear the way he said it, Marie. He meant it. I think he's planning something."

"Don't be ridiculous. My brother isn't smart enough to plan *anything*." She looked at her watch. "If we don't get into the City, we're gonna be late for dinner."

weds.

ok, i got your letter & all the info. seems pretty easy to do.

first let me say that i feel sorry for you lady. it must suck to have some loser druggie creep ruinning your peace & quiet.

i smoke pot myself, its not a big deal. but theres a big difference between smoking a joint once in a while & dealing it. where i live you go to the projects to get your stuff, no one deals out of a house. one time the people on my block heard that someone was in the area trying to sell drugs to their kids & my father formed a group & they beat the living hell out of the guy & torched his car. all i can say is, it worked & he never came back, & the police looked the other way.

which will probably happen this time too. i mean, if this guy is a dealer, everyone knows he is a piece of shit & no one will care what happens to him. i watch plenty of tv, everyone knows that when a dealer gets wacked no one looks too hard for the one who killed him.

bottom line is, lady i respect what you are going thru. don't feel bad about this, the guy knows he is in a dangerous ~~bizness~~ busness & this is going to happen sooner or later. if not you/me then defanitely someone else.

thurs. & fri.

it only takes about 40 mins to get to bloomfield nj from here, an easy ride down the cross brx expwy & into nj & onto the garden state pkwy, when theres no traffic that is.

since i dont start work til noon it was easy to check out the place. letter said this dude 'freddy' doesn't work so had to be careful. first time i drove down the block just to eyeball the house, little tiny house that doesnt fit in. all the other places are nice, small houses too but they look like someone lives in them & takes care of them. freddys place is a pigsty, lawn is in terrible shape & broken flower pots on the steps & alum. siding needs washing & 1 gutter is falling down etc. the van was there, looks like a junk van from that old show 'sandford & son.'

all in all a pigsty, i can see why the neighbors are so pissed off. how can people live like this, its fucking ~~unbeleivable~~ unbelievable.

second time i borrowed my brothers car so no one would notice my car on the street 2 days in a row. but no one was outside anyway, probably all working etc.

i thought maybe i would get a look @ 'freddy' but the windows & doors are shut & you cant see in the windows, & he was not outside the 2 times i drove past.

then i went @ night after work, around 1 am. street is totally deserted etc, very dark exc. for streetlights. nobody even parks on the street, all the little toyotas hondas etc in driveways. but in front of freddys house the van was sticking out of the driveway & someone parked on the front lawn & there was another car parked backward in front of the house. all the houses were dark even freddys but you could hear loud music inside freddys house going boom boom boom even from the street.

sat.

████ ██████ rd. is a quiet deadend. also very very dark which is good.

the street is not far from bloomfield ave which is the main drag thru the town, lots of ~~restarants~~ restuarants, stores, bars etc there with cars parked up & down. so i parked in the parking lot of 1 of the bars which was crowded & walked down ■■■■ ■■■■■■ rd. i wore black pants & sneakers & shirt to camou- fladge myself which i thought was a smart idea. tho i guess peo- ple on the block are now used to freddy getting alot of compa- ny so they wouldnt notice anyway. but better safe than sorry right?

also i brought my dog to take him for a walk. that would make sense, lots of people walk their dogs late @ nite, i even car- ried a pooper scooper.

finally i wore a 'bald wig' that i bought @ the party store, & it was funny i actually looked good in it.

around 11 some kids pull up to the house in a loud car blast- ing hiphop shit music. there all laffing, high, etc. 1 of em gets out, goes round the back of the house & comes back out about 3 mins later. him & his buds drive away with their x or pot or whatever it is.

theres a lite on by freddys back door, so after the kids leave i go back to where my car is parked & leave the dog in there. hes a good dog, he wont bark or anything. then i go back to the house & walk down the driveway to check out the backyard etc.

yard isnt big but theres a shed that its easy to hide behind, plus bushes trees & a fence etc. so that the people in the next block cant see the yard. so i hang out behind the shed & in the next hour about 5 or 6 other people come to the back- door & knock. same thing happens, they go in & come out a few mins later.

well that was enuff research for one nite so i called it quits, but as i was walking down the block back to the car i saw some- one else pull up & get out of the car, the girl was by herself. so i waited for her to come back out & pretended to 'meet' her in the driveway. so i asked her, is this where freddy lives, i need to get some shit. & she says, yeah, he'll have whatever i need. then i asked is it cool in there, & she says yeah, no problem. then i told her that a buddy of mine told me about freddy & i hadnt met him before, was it cool to just go & knock on the door? so she tells me no, there is a different door & different knock every week, this week u have to use the backdoor & knock twice, then wait, then knock once, then wait, then knock three times, then ring the bell, otherwise he wont answer. i said sounds like a lot of fucking work & she laughed & said yeah but its worth it & can you blame the guy, alot of narcs out there who would mess up his biz. & he had to protect himself. which i agreed made sense & she laughed. so i said hey, you look familiar, is your name ronda? & she goes no, its linda, & i say oh sorry, you look like a girl i went to high school with. & she says yeah, all blonds look alike & laughed, & i said catch ya later. & she said cool & left, prob went to get stoned with her friends.

i got back to the car & the bar was still busy, nobody saw me or anything, except for the dog who was sleeping & happy on the backseat.

it was a good info nite all told & i think it should not be too hard to do. i kinda want to get this over with but i dont wanna fuck it up so i am going to be patient.

tues./weds.

the same drill, went to check out the house a couple more times, once around 10 right after work, once before going to work. nothing special, same house etc, no freddy. the house looks ~~deserted~~ desserted, if u didnt know someone lives there u would think it was empty/vacant.

anyhow, i got the place figured out, this weekend i am going to meet freddy darget for the 1st time.

fri.

i remembered what that girl said about having to go to a diff. door & have a diff. knock every week when you needed stuff. so on fri. i borrowed my mothers car (told her i had a date & wanted to impress the girl with a nice cadillac instead of my stupid car) & headed down to jersey again. same drill, i parked the car on the main drag & wore my disguise, then went back to ■■■■ ■■■■■■ road & hid in the backyard.

sure enuff not even ½ hr later two dirtbag guys come walking halfway down the driveway & i hear them knocking @ the side door. the door opens & they go in. but i didnt get the knock 100% down, i thought it was 3 knocks, then wait, then 2 knocks, then wait, then 1 knock, but i wasnt sure. so those 2 guys leave in a little while & i keep hanging out until 2 more people come, i think a guy & a girl this time, & it turns out i had the knock right.

so when they left it was my turn. i was nervous but not super nervous, to tell you the truth i have bought pot in plenty of places & it is easy, only thing to watch for is narcs. no one wants any trouble, the dealer wants his $$ & you want your pot, you just go in, get your stuff & leave. that is to say, you both want the same things, & neither of you wants to get busted, so you are both careful.

i waited about 5 mins & then walked up the driveway just to see if there were any headlites coming down the road. none were so i did the knock & waited.

the door opens up & there is this guy, long hair, a couple of ~~tatoos~~ ~~tattooes~~ tattoos & what a fucking speciman he is, strung out. so i say hey & he says whats up.

i say linda told me he might have some stuff i am looking for, is it cool?

he says, i dont think ive seen you here before.

& i say, no, but linda told me it was cool.

so he says come in & we will talk.

i go in & jesus christ the place is a fucking slum, shit everywhere & it stinks like hell. im not the neatest & my mother is always bitching me out about my room being a pigsty but thats because shes there to clean up, if i lived by myself i would take care of everything. but this guy lives like an animal, theres ½ eaten food everywhere & the stuffing is pulled out of the couch & the windows & mirrors are dirty. theres mirrors all over the table in the kitchen & living room, def. for doing coke lines.

so i say thanks man, can you hook me up with about 4 hits of x.

he says, it'll cost you 60.

i say no problem, i have the money.

he says let me see your drivers license.

i say what?

he goes, let me see your wallet.

i say i dont have it with me, i never carry a wallet, but i have the $$ in my pocket & i take out 60 bucks, 3 20s to show that i have the cash for the x.

he goes, your not a narc are you man?

so i say, shit bro, defanitely not, why do u think that.

he says, you look it with that big gut and shaved head.

i say, i'd never be a fucking pig, theyre all assholes, they brake more laws than they protect & what i do with my life is none of there fucking ~~bizness~~ busness.

he laffs & says, no fucking shit man, all they care about is hassling people.

so i say, my girlfriend really wants the x, she gives a much better blowjob when she does a hit & we are going away tomorrow so can i please get it man?

he looks me up & down & says, alright man, it looks like i can trust u.

& i think but i dont say, yah well u can trust me not to narc on u thats for sure. cause its the truth, i have no plans of dropping a dime on him.

he says wait here & goes up the stairs on the other side of the living room. i look around but not too closely cuz the place is grossing me out & i just want to get out of there.

he comes back 2 mins later w/ 4 hits. i give him the 60 bucks & say thanks, i appreciate it, this is much easier than getting it @ clubs in the city.

& he says, thats what im here for.

so i say, is it cool to come back for more next week?

& he says yah, ask linda, she'll tell you what the knock is. or call my machine on weds 973-■■■-■■■■. that'll tell you my hours for next week.

i say, ok no problem, how late can i show up, i dont wanna wake you up or nothing.

& he says the latest i open the door this week is 3, after that i dont answer, so get here before 3 or not @ all. call the machine on weds for info about next week.

i say thanks & for some reason i go to shake his hand. he looks @ me funny like im a fucking weirdo yuppie & says never mind with the handshakes man, this aint corporate america & the only people i shake hands with are my friends & you aint a friend.

so i think fuck you, youll be fucking dead soon anyway, but i just say cool & leave.

i met up with 3 guys @ a club & sold them the x @ a good profit so everything worked out just fine.

sat.

on sat. morning i realized i had a problem. i told freddy that linda was my friend but what would happen if linda came back soon & he asked her about me. she'd say she didnt know me etc. & he would either get pissed & not let me back in or he'd know something was up & get ~~susspiscious~~ susspicious.

the odds seem in my favor cuz freddy is so fucking fried & wasted from what i can tell he might not even remember i was there. but still i think shit, i gotta do this soon. i was gonna wait til next week but what if linda shows up in the meantime & narcs me out.

so i drive into the city, times square that day & i get myself a fake ID from pensylvannia with a phoney name & adress. this way if he asks again i can show it. it even has my pic on it with the disguise. i had to change into the disguise in a mens room in a restuarant near times square, i went in looking one way & came out looking another way like super spy.

i was nervous all day but i needed a weapon of some sort. just to catch freddy off guard. i am bigger & stronger than he is, he looks so weak & out of it. it had to be something small & easy to carry & hide, i decided on a brick paver. i bought six at the garden center & left them in the car.

i figured i needed an allibi for the nite so i purposely hung with some friends until the club closed at 2 am. a friend (i wont say his name) picked me up & dropped me off @ home & i made sure he saw me go into the house etc. i had left my car parked a few blocks away earlier in the day & so when he was gone i walked & picked up my car & headed to freddys house.

i got into bloomfield @ 240 or so. i wanted to be the last person freddy saw that nite, this way if he didnt answer the door nobody would be the wiser. this time i parked almost 20 blocks away in a motel parking lot, which i scoped out during 1 of my trips. it took 10 mins to walk to freddys house so it was 250 when i got there.

it was a quiet nite on ■■■■ ■■■■■■ rd & no one was entering or leaving freddys house. i had the paver in the pocket of my jacket. i went to the side door & did the knock & freddy opens the door.

he recognizes me & says whats up, thought you were going away this weekend.

i said yeah but it got postponed til tomorrow & we did all our X last nite, we need some more, do you have any?

he says yah, come in.

so i go in & i say, i brought my i.d. tonite if you wanna see it.

so he says, show it to me.

so i reach into my pocket & show him. its a good fake, he has no idea.

he says how many hits you need.

i say 6.

alright he says, wait here. then he turns & starts walking, i guess to go upstairs & get the X.

thats when i pull out the paver & smash it on the back of his head. he goes down & i jump on top of him, hit him w/ the paver a few more times. he hardly even struggles. i dont wanna get blood & shit on me so thats when i start choking him, i just squeeze & squeeze & before you know it, no more Freddy. it was easy, i just pretended i was squeezing the neck of that asshole who thinks he is gonna be my brother in law.

i looked @ my watch, it was 303 am.

i figure he must have $$ in the house, so i put on the gloves & go looking & there is almost 4 grand in the dresser draws in his bedroom. so i pocket it, might as well use the cash for something useful right?

i put the paver back in my pocket & the time is like 310.

i look out the door & the coast is clear. i walk back to my car, pretending i have a limp JUST IN CASE anyone sees me, they will say it was a guy who limped on his left leg.

i got the car from the motel lot. on the way home i drove over the g washington bridge/hudson river & dropped the pavers in. when i get home, no one even hears me since i sleep on the 1st floor & have my own entrance & all the other bed-rooms are on the 2nd floor.

i cut up the ID into tiny pieces. & the clothes from that nite too. each day for the next few weeks i will throw out a few bits & pieces here & there, no one will be able to trace anything.

so thats it lady, your asshole druggie nieghbor is history. the fucker deserved it, a loser who lives in shit up to his ears & doesnt even have the descency to shake someones hand.

C

Joseph Castro

"OK, guys. It's been great talking to you today. Before I head out, does anyone have any questions?"

A boy raised his hand tentatively.

"Sure, what is it, buddy?"

"I'm just wondering how many people you've shot."

The teacher reacted with horror. "Ethan! That's not an appropriate question to ask Detective Castro."

Joe smiled. "It's OK, Mrs. Washington. It's important for kids to understand what police officers do, and what they don't do." He turned to the class and concocted a story he thought would be plausible.

"The truth is, in my entire career I've shot only one person. It was a man who was robbing a store and who had beaten up the owner very badly. But even though he did some terrible things to an innocent man, I wouldn't have shot him if I didn't have to. Police officers and detectives carry guns *only* to protect themselves and other people. Using our guns is our last resort. In this particular case, the man was shooting at me and my partner and also threatening to hurt other people in the store. My basic point is: Guns are for protection only. Don't buy into what you see on TV and in the movies. Shooting people isn't cool. It's a horrible experience that you never forget."

Mrs. Washington beamed at Detective Castro with approval.

This was one part of his job that Joe Castro liked. Most of the other guys on the squad (and now the girls on the squad too, thanks to the politically correct bullshit of a certain female New York senator) resented having to talk to kids about staying off drugs, out of gangs, and off the streets. They were rough-and-tumble, hard-edged guys who'd seen every type of brutality and perversity as they climbed the ranks to detective, and their experiences hadn't given them the gentle understanding and sweetness of outlook that is helpful when dealing with children—even the savvy, street-smart, sexually active children of New York City.

He and Jesus Montoya ended up doing most of the drug talks because Joe's partner, Nick Lang, preferred defensive driving school, where it was easier to meet pretty, eligible, dumb girls who'd gotten tickets for putting on their make-up while speeding along the Long Island Expressway at 85 miles an hour. And that was fine—he and Nick spent enough time together as it was.

Aside from Lang, Montoya was the closest thing Joe had to a friend. Montoya was from a huge, extended Latino family and had four kids of his own, so he knew how to relate to them. *The fucking spics have their problems*, Joe thought, *but they know the value of children and family*. In fact, it was hard not to admire Montoya, who had a tranquillity about him that Joe could never have achieved.

Joe found it ironic that as a child he'd liked talking to adults more than to kids his own age, and now, as an adult, he preferred spending time around children. As a kid, he'd thought (wrongly, as it turned out) that adults were much more sensible, and had much more to say, than the stupid kids he played stickball with. After he joined the police force and realized that adults were without exception twisted, brutal, conniving, manipulative, lying, and selfish, he found that he enjoyed the company of kids more. He had two young nieces and two teenage nephews, all of whom worshipped him. The girls bragged about him to their friends, and the boys saw him as a model of strength and cool.

He'd begun coaching Little League baseball five years earlier when one of his nephews had suddenly found himself without a coach (the previous volunteer had been wound too tightly and had suffered a heart attack during the fifth inning of the season's first game). Joe's nephew had been heartbroken that he might not play ball, so Joe had stepped up to the plate.

There was something energizing about reliving his former glories by teaching his tips and techniques to the younger generation. And now he was trying something new: coaching the girls' soccer team at the Catholic school. He had mixed feelings about that. He was resentful that Title IX had drained important money away from the boys' sports to fund what he considered ridiculous girls' teams, such as the girls' weightlifting team and the girls' hockey league. But the church rec committee had begged him, and his nieces, who'd wanted to be on the team, had done the same. So, after asking Father R for advice, he'd given in.

Accepting the gig as the girls' soccer coach was part of a conscious attempt to lift himself out of a funk into which he'd fallen over the last couple of years. One of the things that so bothered him about humanity, and about the hundreds of drunken, stupid, ignorant, malicious adults he'd arrested over the years, was their complete inability to look at their lives, to step outside themselves and say, "I really need to get my life together. Maybe I should stop smoking crack, stop beating my kids, and start putting food on the table. Maybe I should quit running stop signs, speeding, and selling drugs in school zones." But no, they never stepped outside themselves. They went on doing crack, beating their kids, and zooming around residential streets like Jeff Gordon.

Joe Castro didn't want to be that kind of guy, the typical pathetic loser who makes the same mistakes over and over again. His job took so much out of him, and it would have been easy to let it take over his life, to let it lead him down that same spiral staircase that caused problems in his weaker colleagues. But he was a fighter. He wanted to be better than he was. And Father R was trying to help him with that.

Father R was trying to help him with his attitude towards women, too. But no matter how Joe tried, he couldn't stop himself from resenting the pushy women of New York, who refused to accept the simple truth that *they cannot do the same things men can do*. Some of them actually applied for jobs in the fire department—the fire department, where you have to carry 250-pound people five flights down a rickety ladder while a building blazes around you—and they sued when they didn't pass the tests. It was unbelievable, just fucking unbelievable.

Women were supposed to be soft and nurturing. They were supposed to take care of the house, their husband, and their kids, not fight crime or fires. They were truly skilled in the domestic areas, much more so than men. And men were skilled in things like construction and chasing the bad guys (yes, bad *guys*, because everyone knows women don't go around raping men or murdering rival gang members). Why couldn't society just let each sex do what it did best?

It had worked that way for years. Joe's father had been a detective, too. He and Joe had gone to ballgames while his mother and two sisters had stayed home, cooked, sewn, and cleaned. When the girls had asked Joe Sr. if they could go to the ballgame with him and Joe Jr., Pop had laughed and said, "Girls, you'd be bored." When they'd asked him if they could go to work with him, the way Joe Jr. sometimes did, Pop had said, "The station isn't the place for you, girls. Stay home and play with your dolls."

And his sisters hadn't complained, because they knew their complaints would fall on deaf ears. So they'd stayed home and played with their dolls, as instructed, and they'd been spared the horrors of seeing what police see, the kinds of subhuman beings they chase down, arrest, and process every day. And they were better off for it. It's easier to go on living when you don't know what's happening in the world just beyond your street corner.

If only his wives had been more like his sisters. Both of them had started out fine, but they'd changed almost as soon as he'd placed the wedding ring on their finger. He should have known better than to marry New York girls; everyone knows they turn into loud, nagging, abrasive harpies who live to ride your ass. Sharon had been an A student in high school; she'd been pretty and popular, and she felt lucky to have Joe, whom all the girls considered a hottie. They married young, and he thought children would follow soon thereafter, but Sharon had other ideas. She loved her sales job, and she started spending more and more time away from home, leaving him to eat take-out meals and turn to other women for the sex he was missing while Sharon was on the road. She kept putting off having kids, then admitted one night that she might not want them at all. Things spiraled downhill; they fought, argued, and slapped. She freaked when he stopped hiding the fact that other women found him attractive and that he took them up on their offers. When they divorced, she thought she had him by the balls—but he got the house, and thanks to her hefty salary, she got no alimony. It didn't hurt that Joe had helped the divorce judge drywall his basement a couple of years earlier.

He wasn't about to make the same mistakes with Eileen that he'd made with Sharon. He'd been too easy on Sharon, hadn't kept her on enough of a leash, hadn't kept enough tabs on her comings and goings, hadn't wanted to deal with her increasing bitchiness when he came home from another day of shootings, stabbings, and mutilations. But Eileen would toe the line.

And she did, for a while. She kept a nice house, always looked good, and liked sex. But she was critical. God, was she critical. He wasn't romantic enough, she complained. Was it so much to ask for a card on Valentine's Day, Christmas, her birthday? Why didn't he ever bring her perfume or flowers? Why didn't they go into the City more, see shows, go to the movies, have dinner? Why didn't they talk the way they used to?

After a couple of years he could no longer stand Eileen yammering in his ear, her constant nagging and complaining. *You don't know what I go through every fucking day of my life*, he screamed in his mind. *You sit in a nice house and have lunch with your girlfriends while I arrest men who rape two-year-olds and Chinese drug dealers who blow away entire families with machine guns. You don't realize how fucking good you have it, so just shut up, shut up, shut up shut the fuck up!* Yes, he'd had to swat her a few times, swat her like the gnat she could be, buzzing around his head, annoying him, making him feel overwhelmed and dizzy, but he hadn't hit her hard. And she'd deserved it. None of it would have happened if she'd just left him the fuck alone.

She was another one who thought she could get money out of him, steal his detective's pension, his house, his other assets. How wrong she was.

Women complain that men don't want kids, he thought. *And here I am...I want kids. I've been married twice, and I still don't have them. And I think I need them. They're the only things that will stop me from sliding down further and further and further.*

The NYPD shrink, who made a habit of missing the obvious and whom he'd been forced to see monthly after the incident in which he'd "accidentally" shot a fleeing suspect through the heart instead of the leg, blamed Joe's occasional drinking for the breakup of his marriages, but Joe knew there was more to it than that. It was years of seeing the worst of humanity day in, day out. Images were burned into his mind...images of scarred and scabbed children, decapitated corpses, back alley abortions...images he couldn't shake. The alcohol helped blur the images and conceal the truth: that Joseph Castro, Jr. could do nothing to improve the world.

Maybe he couldn't improve the world, but he *could* take advantage of the few fringe benefits offered by his job. Nearly a decade on the force had shown Joe that a policeman could wield a tremendous amount of discretionary power. If you stopped someone for driving too fast, you made the choice: give him a ticket or let him go. If you caught kids selling drugs, you decided whether to give them a lecture or a court date. And if you set yourself up as an authority figure—one who should be respected, one who should not be fucked with—you could reap some of the benefits of the godforsaken job, where nobody appreciated you and nobody cared what you sacrificed to get scumbags off the streets. You could walk out of a restaurant without paying—didn't the owner owe it to you for keeping his place safe? You could drink at a bar without paying, too—wasn't it the barkeep's way of acknowledging that your presence in his joint made it a more desirable place to hang out? You could fuck a hooker and not pay her—what was she going to do about it, call to report you? It was the least she could do, a sort of thank you for not tossing her ass in jail. If you were underpaid for all you did and sacrificed, wasn't it all right to find alternative sources of income, which maybe weren't completely above board, but which didn't hurt anyone? And so what if you drove too fast or, occasionally, drunk? Other people drove too fast, or drunk, all the time, and they got away with it, thanks to hotshot lawyers, incompetent cops, or just pure luck. So why couldn't you, too, get away with it—you, who'd given everything, including your wives and your hopes for a family—to serve and protect?

And he *was* getting away with all of it. But why was he feeling worse every day? That's the question the shrink was trying to get him to answer, but there hadn't been any breakthroughs. And he didn't want there to be. He hated that fucking shrink with his annoying smirk and bony arms. He much preferred talking to Father R.

He was still going to the same church to which he'd gone with his family as a kid. It had changed, of course. Once predominantly Italian and Irish, it was now crawling with Latinos. But he felt comfortable at St. Elizabeth's. He'd spent many a Sunday during his childhood serving as an altar boy, and he had fond memories of church picnics and kindly priests who'd coached the basketball and hockey teams. He still volunteered his time as peacekeeper and security guard when the church sponsored carnivals—riffraff never lost an opportunity to crash a decent neighborhood at carnival time—and he sometimes spoke to the CYO on the dangers of drugs, guns, gangs, and peer pressure.

Father R saw in one day what the shrink hadn't seen in more than a year of sessions. A few months earlier, Father R had been present as Joe addressed a group of jittery, testosterone-crazed teenage boys from the Catholic school about careers in law enforcement. Normally he would have stopped all horseplay with a glance at the perpetrators, but he was too weary to deviate from the talk he'd planned in his head, a talk he'd given dozens of times. The boys didn't pay much attention and dispersed noisily when the talk was over.

"Unruly bunch today, hey Joe?"

"Yeah, what can you do?" Joe had murmured.

"You never had any trouble doing something before."

"Just seemed like too much trouble today."

"You haven't been yourself lately, Joe. Are you OK?"

"Yeah, just busy at work."

"You know, my door is always open if you ever want to talk. I don't mean the confessional door...I mean my office door."

"I'm OK, Father. Really."

But a few days later, after he'd given a Manhattan prostitute a black eye, he'd shown up in Father R's office, and the conversation had begun.

It had been Father R who'd talked him into coaching the girls' soccer team. "Joe, you're stuck in a different era. It's the twenty-first century now. Women aren't kept chained up in their homes any more. You have to do something to change your outlook. Start with your strengths and work with them. You like working with kids, and the kids on your teams love you. But all the work you've done is with boys. God has given you the opportunity to start working with girls. If being their coach doesn't show you they're wonderful human beings with dreams and hopes and personalities, just like boys are, I don't know what will. Just do it, Joe. It'll be the best thing for you, and it'll help you forget some of those horrible cases you're working on. Please say yes, Joe. We need you. *They* need you."

Joe had reluctantly agreed. Those girls took some getting used to. Some of them were real tomboys who wanted to be great soccer players, while others were more concerned about scraping their nail polish or losing the various oddities that held their hair in place. But that little Jessie was a hell of a center, and he saw Marlys and Julietta as potentially excellent halfbacks. Teresita couldn't move to save her life, but she seemed to be getting the hang of goalie, and Paula, God love her, was useless but funny as hell.

It was a start. And Father R had been right. Coaching the girls was helping him keep his mind off the horrors of the job and his most recent case, at least for now. The case itself wasn't going very well, but he'd come up with a way to get closure on it, and he thought it would work. He thought of himself as doing it for the girls on his soccer team.

A

What a hassle getting to and from Throgs Neck. Perpetual construction on the Throgs Neck Bridge. But a deal's a deal.

Throgs Neck, NY: A remote corner of the Bronx. Far from upscale Riverdale on the Hudson, but a hell of a step up from Morris Park and the South Bronx. Tiny little houses on top of one another, some with a small patch of grass separating them from the sidewalk, others sitting almost on the street. Looks like the houses were one-family when they were built, probably in the 1930s and 40s, but now every house has dormers or other additions, probably put up hastily so that divorced loser kids can move back in with their parents. Most of the additions look like they're illegal or go against zoning regs. Guess the politicians in Throgs Neck are as crooked as they are everywhere else in this city.

Most of the houses have driveways, but the streets are still clogged with parked cars and SUVs. The driveways were meant to accommodate one or two cars, but each house, with its two or three apartments, must have five or six cars total.

Roger Borelli has the upstairs apartment in what has to be an illegal three-family, probably owned by some landlord who uses the rent to pay the mortgage on a much nicer house with much more property in a much better place. Hard to believe you can pack three apartments into a tiny expanded Cape, but that's what 6 ■■■■■■ ■■ is. You could reach your hand out a window on the side of Roger's house and touch the house next door.

With so many cars parked on a street, it's easy to blend in, especially when you're driving the most nondescript of all cars, a dark blue Chevy.

Roger goes to bed late and gets up early. His life couldn't be more normal. Work, go out drinking with friends, come home, take a shower, hang out with his girlfriend, go to bed, wake up and do it all over again. The guy must have plenty of energy, to be hanging with his buddies or screwing his girlfriend, until one or two a.m., and then leave for work by seven. Good for him.

I've seen Roger's type my whole life. Guys like him are everywhere. Maybe I'm even a little like him myself. You can tell from his walk, his demeanor: self-confident, a little cocky. The kind of guy that girls like. The type who probably would never hit you, but just might if you pushed him too far. Definitely a temper. One night I heard him and his girlfriend screaming at each other. The apartment windows were shut, but you could have heard the argument on the next block. A couple mornings later he left for work and saw that someone had parked too tightly behind his truck, squeezing it in. He kicked the door of the offending car and punched the driver's side window. It didn't break.

The guy's oblivious to the world around him. Wait, no. That's not right. He's oblivious to other guys. But he checks out every girl who passes him, especially the hot ones. Who can blame him? The girls check him out, too. He's good looking, in good shape. Sometimes he talks to them, flirts a little, smiles, teases. Maybe he's just making sure that he still "has it." He'll be in his thirties soon. His hair will start thinning, and his belly will start growing. Might as well enjoy turning heads while he still can. Can't hold it against the guy.

Can't hold it against him that he wants to go out drinking with his friends, either. He walks into a place and everyone knows him. It's all hail fellow, well met. His tastes run from the blue collar to the downright seedy: bars, pubs, taverns, and local joints. Lacee's is a strip club filled with lowlifes. Scamps is filled with a bunch of cheap whores who go home with a different guy every night. The Lido has strip shows, lap dances, and hookers and drugs in the back room. City Lites is an "upscale" club filled with big hair and gold chains. It's the only club he takes his girl-friend/fiancée to.

You're right about this guy, I think. Selfish, self-centered. Primary concern: Having a good time, copping a feel, getting laid. He's one of those guys who likes cheap whorish girls. The kind of guy who thinks it's cool, enviable, to be on a first-name basis with the dancers, the strippers, the skags who get ten bucks for a blowjob. Same type of guy whose life goal is to star in a porn flick, surrounded by siliconed, botoxed, drugged-up girls who take turns sucking his dick.

He's the ring leader, the alpha male. His friends look up to him, defer to him. He's a benevolent dictator, though. Smiles and laughs for everyone. There's one guy in his group, I heard them call him "Scooter," definitely a nerdish guy. Under most normal circumstances, Scooter wouldn't be hanging around with this cool, popular, closely knit group of pals. They throw their arms around Scooter, egg him on to do stupid things, then laugh at him when he does. But they're not mocking him. They like him, you can tell. And he likes them. He's like a grateful puppy allowed to sit at his masters' feet.

If you told Roger Borelli that someone had been following him around for two weeks, he'd say, "No way. I'd have noticed." But he *hasn't* noticed. The only things he notices are tits and ass. I have neither. I just blend in, one of the guys sipping coffee at the diner in the morning, having a drink at a nightclub and chatting with some single girls, or sitting on the other end of the bar having a beer, watching the game, and not bothering anyone.

I guess the guy isn't really any more likable, or hateful, than any one of the twelve million other people living in New York City. In my own life I'd probably be able to tolerate him. But this isn't about me. A deal's a deal.

* * *

It was easy, mostly because Roger's life was so predictable. Friday night was boys' night out. Saturday was date night. So a Friday would be the best time to do it. I didn't want to do it in his apartment. The street was much too busy, people always coming and going.

The Lido would be the best place. Scamps would be second best. I didn't want to do it at Lacee's—too well lit, the front door on a service road to the Throgs Neck Expressway.

I bought fresh comfortable clothes (jeans, a sweatshirt) and some cheap shoes at Kmart that I'd have no trouble throwing away. It hurts to throw away expensive shoes.

Luck was on my side. He left his apartment around 10:30 p.m., looking freshly showered. I followed at a discreet distance as he made his way to the Lido. The place is always crowded on weekends, but he managed to find a spot in the back of the lot, near a guardrail that prevents cars from plunging into a sewer runoff behind the property.

I drove away and joy rode around the Bronx for a couple of hours. Just enough time to let Roger get a few drinks under his belt.

At 1 a.m., I pulled out a cell phone I'd stolen from some kid on the N train when he wasn't looking. I dialed Roger's cell phone number, knowing he'd answer on the first or second ring. That's the thing about cell phones. Everyone who owns one thinks they're important, thinks they'd keel over dead if they missed a phone call. So they stop whatever they're doing to answer the phone.

"Hey," he said. "Hold on a second, there's loud music, I'm going outside...hold on, I'm almost there...one more second...OK, I'm outside. Hey."

"Mr. Borelli?"

"Yeah, this is Roger Borelli."

"This is Detective William Harper from the Throgs Neck PD."

"What's wrong?"

"I've been assigned to your case."

"My case?"

"Haven't you been assaulted by Leo Lentricchia?"

Yes, I did learn that your name is Leo Lentricchia. It's against the rules, but I needed the information. It was easy to follow your sister home one night, look at the mailbox to figure out the family's last name, and figure out your name, too.

"Well, yeah, I have, but I didn't file charges or anything. I didn't even know the police knew about it..."

"Mr. Borelli, we're pursuing this for a reason. We think Leo Lentricchia is dangerous. I need to talk with you in person."

Roger hesitated a moment. "OK. Sure. It's a little weird though, the guy is actually gonna be my brother-in-law this time next year. I've been trying not to make a big deal about it, but there's a side of me that's been, well, kind of afraid."

"The sooner we talk, the better. Are you at home right now?"

"No, I'm out with some friends. But I can meet you at my house."

"Where are you?"

"I'm at the Lido Bar on Tremont Ave."

"I'm not far from there. I'll meet you there in ten minutes."

"That sounds OK. How about by the jukebox?"

"Too loud. We need to talk where it's quiet. The parking lot is better."

"OK, how about my truck? It's a black Explorer."

"What's the license plate?"

"███ ███."

"All right, see you in ten minutes. Stay outside in case I need to call you back." I didn't want him going back inside and telling his friends he was meeting a "detective" in the parking lot.

"No problem, I want to get a pack of cigarettes from the truck anyway."

Within five minutes I was approaching the Lido. I pulled onto a side street and parked, then walked the rest of the way. This Borelli character wasn't too bright. He hadn't asked how I'd gotten his cell phone number, or why I was doing detective work at one o'clock in the morning.

Borelli was sitting in his truck smoking a cigarette, the window open. I walked up and flashed what could have been a badge.

"Roger Borelli? Detective William Harper."

"Hey," he said. He seemed anxious as he shook my hand. "Is this an OK place to talk?"

"Yeah," I said, climbing into the passenger seat.

"You guys work late hours, huh?"

"Crime doesn't happen just nine to five, Mr. Borelli."

"Ha-ha," he laughed, nervously. "I'm sorry, Detective, I'm a little nervous. I guess I've been on edge about Leo. He's crazy, I'm telling you. He has a hair up his ass about me, and I've never done anything to him. Have you met him? Do you know what his eyes look like? He's like Luka Brazzi on *The Godfather*, just a big dumb...."

I reached into my jacket, placed the gun (with silencer) against his temple, and pulled the trigger.

Roger slumped down onto his seat. I grabbed the wallet in his back pocket and put it into my own. Three minutes later I was heading south on the Throgs Neck Expressway. Within ten minutes I was crossing the bridge and flinging the gun and the wallet (minus a few hundred dollars in cash) into Long Island

Sound. I'd bought the gun on the streets of the South Bronx years earlier, and the guy who'd sold it to me was long dead.

Dr. John Althorp

If he lived to be a million, Dr. John Althorp would never understand why it was so unacceptable to lament declining educational standards.

Throughout the country, students were leaving high school unable to read, unable to find Iraq on a map, unable to write a cogent sentence with a noun and a verb. They thought Paris was the capital of Europe and William Shakespeare was a highly-paid producer of hiphop music. They went to college because their parents forced them to, or because they wanted to make a lot of money and saw a college degree as a step toward achieving that goal. In the twenty-first century, Dr. Althorp had decided, education wasn't a goal in itself. It was simply a means to an end.

But that wasn't the worst part of it. With all the educational activism in recent years, cities were getting more money than ever for their schools, but they were still turning out ignorant students who went on to college unprepared and unmotivated. Those same kids drove expensive cars and wore overpriced sneakers but cried over the price of textbooks; didn't work because Mom and Dad gave them money, but complained about the reading load in a literature course; and promptly shut their minds to any theory or critical thinking activity that instructors didn't aggressively link to the "real world."

Yes, the world was a different place than it had been when he'd started teaching at Mendham College in the late 1970s. Then, there had still been some social conscience, as well as some value placed on learning for its own sake. Across the schools of study, from arts and humanities to sciences and family studies, the faculty had shared a common goal: to pass on to students the cultural literacy that defines an educated person. Students read Plato, Aristotle, and Sophocles whether they wanted to or not. They memorized parts of *The Communist Manifesto*. They read every one of the Canterbury Tales, not just a few of them, and they read them in Middle English. They didn't graduate with a degree in the arts without reading all of Shakespeare's tragedies, comedies, histories, and sonnets. They didn't get that piece of sheepskin unless they could distinguish a Manet from a Monet, and a Mahler from a Mozart.

That was then—students started their freshman year knowing how to write a paragraph and how to read a book. This was now—students arrived at Mendham worrying about alcohol first and their studies second. In the old days, students felt a pronounced sense of embarrassment when they overdid it and got drunk in public. Today they bragged about it and planned to do it again soon.

He was a traditionalist, but not a Luddite. Far from it, in fact. He wasn't in love with computers, true, but in the 1980s he sensed that they were the wave of the future, and he'd been instrumental in securing funding for the school's lavishly furnished computer lab. He was skeptical of the e-world, but he supported cross-disciplinary courses and seminars on Net-related topics and trends. Having witnessed the decline of personal ethics and social responsibility, he'd worked long and hard to create a Center for Ethical Studies at the college.

He'd made more than his share of compromises over the years, but there were some things on which he refused to compromise. Mendham had always been a fine school, and if he had anything to say about it, it was going to remain that way. That meant focusing on core values, on what had always worked, and not being distracted by every flash-in-the-pan politically correct trend and educational fad.

Most of the faculty—men, and a few women, with whom he'd taught for twenty-five years before he'd accepted the Dean's position—were on his side. They were united in their beliefs, their standards, and their lack of patience for nonsense and pablum. They didn't believe in giving a passing grade to an underachieving athlete just so he could stay on the team. They wouldn't give any paper with grammar or punctuation errors above a "C." And they wouldn't sacrifice core material in any of their courses (literature, philosophy, music, history) to focus on the work of second- or third-rate practitioners whom desperate graduate students were trying resurrect in an effort to make a name for themselves. College was a place to study the major poets, not the minor poets. It was a place to study Spenser and Dickens, not Margaret Atwood and Alice Walker.

This didn't mean the faculty discouraged students from pursuing other interests or exploring other avenues, if the students were interested in doing so. In fact, some of the English faculty handed out alternate reading lists by secondary figures and encouraged papers on those minor, but interesting, works. But in a fifteen-week semester, there was simply too much to cover to waste precious classroom time on the minors.

Maintaining the standards would be easy if he were just allowed to do so. But he felt assaulted on all sides. The English department was feeling pressure to vastly expand the canon to include unworthy figures. The history department was rapidly becoming a department of historical trivia as professors spent too much time talking about the negligible contributions of particular ethnic groups. The philosophy department was getting a lot of heat for focusing too much on Western civilization, despite the fact that the United States and all its institutions were founded on a distinctly Western model. The list could go on and on.

John took off his glasses and rubbed his eyes. The charges to dismantle the curriculum and rebuild it on academic politics and nonsense were led by a few young scholars who knew exactly how to play the game for personal advantage. History had Jennifer Steinhaus, who made a stink every year because the U.S. and European history textbooks didn't have enough coverage of women's place in history. Art had the extremely annoying Peter Shafer, who spent half his time bringing freaky performance artists to campus and the other half screaming about discrimination against gays and lesbians. English had the sneaky and underhanded Annette Bain, who would have sold her own mother into slavery for a tenure-track position at Yale, Harvard, or Columbia. Wasn't it funny, John thought, that these up-and-coming "social activist" scholars (using the quotes in his mind) should set their sights on faculty positions at the schools that most embodied social and intellectual stratification? But none of them saw the irony.

And another battle was looming on the horizon. Somehow, when he wasn't looking, a few members of the English Department, led by Annette Bain of course, had begun plotting the dismantling of the six courses required of all English majors at Mendham College. For more than sixty years, English B.A.'s had left the college strongly grounded in poetry from *The Dream of the Rood* through T.S. Eliot, in the novel from Samuel Richardson through Ernest Hemingway, and in the drama from the miracle plays through Harold Pinter. They'd read everything they'd needed to read to become educated, well-rounded editors, publishers, writers, teachers. It was a tough 18 credits, taught by some of the department's best and brightest, and it had always worked.

Now, suddenly, it wasn't good enough. The questions being asked by the committee were all fatuous in the extreme. Where were the women in these courses? (Apparently, Christina Rossetti, Jane Austen, and George Eliot didn't count.) Where were the African-Americans? (Lorraine Hansberry, Frederick Douglass, Richard Wright, Zora Neale Hurston...apparently they didn't count, either.) How could the department, in this era of religious and ethnic diversity, require students to read excerpts from the King James Bible without also requiring them to read excerpts from the *Bhagavad Gita* and the Upanishads? Where was deconstruction, structuralism, and feminist theory? Where were the queer texts? Why weren't Sandra Cisneros and Amy Tan accorded the same respect as Eudora Welty and Flannery O'Connor? Why did we continue to teach writers whom biographers had exposed as homophobic, racist, or anti-Semitic?

The answer to these questions couldn't have been more simple. "My dear colleagues," he wanted to say, "Everyone and everything that *should* be taught, *is* being taught. Everything else is secondary. So please shut up and go back to teaching your courses. Worry more about your students and less about your political agendas."

Of course, he couldn't say any of this. His job was to sit there and listen, and listen, and listen, his guts twisting in irritation and impatience.

He'd been gathering support for keeping the traditional curriculum in the English department, and he was fairly sure the vote would to go his way. But Annette Bain was working equally hard to obliterate everything Mendham College had represented for more than a century. Annette Bain, who loudly badmouthed every Republican who'd ever walked the earth. Annette Bain, who'd published an incomprehensible, poorly written feminist "analysis" of some Victorian nobody who'd published a few horrible poems that had never been read by anyone except Annette Bain. Annette Bain, whose white male students always seemed to receive much lower grades than her female, African-American, or Latino students. Annette Bain, who gave "A" grades to student papers that were riddled with grammatical errors but contained "wonderful ideas." Annette Bain, who didn't give a rat's ass about any Mendham College student who refused to become one of her groupies. Annette Bain, whose anger, animosity, and spite were hidden behind a petite, well-sculpted body and pretty smile.

And to think that he was planning to vote in favor of granting her tenure! He certainly didn't like Annette Bain, but she'd played the tenure game exceedingly well, and she'd almost single-handedly raised the profile of the Mendham College English Department in the literary studies community. The fact that he didn't agree with her politically didn't mean she shouldn't be granted tenure.

Still, the battle lines were drawn. She'd be at today's meeting, smiling sweetly, speaking cogently, putting forth her position as though she were God Herself decreeing curriculum from on high. They'd chat a bit before and afterwards, to show they held no personal animosity toward each other and *completely respected* each other's positions. Then they'd leave the meeting, both wishing the other dead.

He looked at his watch. Almost 2 p.m. Time to head over to Mission Hall for the meeting. He put on his jacket (yes, he still wore a jacket and tie every day, believing educators should set a model for their students), grabbed his satchel, and shut his office door behind him.

"Marianne," he said to his secretary, "I'll be at the curriculum meeting in Mission until about five, and then I'm heading home."

He looked in the lazy susan where Marianne left phone messages for him. It was empty. "No calls?"

"Quiet afternoon, John. A man called for you twice, but he didn't leave his name either time. Said he'll call you back tomorrow."

John wondered for half a second who the caller might have been. Probably some other administrator, maybe even a golf buddy. Well, it didn't matter. He had bigger things to worry about now, like the fate of a wonderful English literature program. "Well, good night, Marianne. See you tomorrow."

Jesse Garanowicz /
Teddy Boyle

Teddy entered the small bedroom he used as a library. The computer was already on—he never turned it off. With a few clicks of his mouse he was simultaneously in a chatroom, surfing the Web, checking his e-mail, and reading the posts on his newsgroups.

The first e-mail he read was from one of his friends, a recluse who lived in Montana (or, at least, said he lived in Montana) and who spent even more time surfing the Web than Teddy did. "Surfer Dude," as he called himself, was a master of finding sites with of-age models who looked much younger than their seventeen or eighteen years. Teddy smiled at the irony. So many kids in their teens made themselves up to appear much older. The girls wore all kinds of make-up, and the boys got all sorts of tattoos or military haircuts, so they could pass for 21. Not the kids on these sites, though. With the help of the photographers, they did everything they could to appear prepubescent. Knowing that they were actually legal killed the fantasy somewhat, if Teddy thought about it too much. But that kept it all nice and above board. This was a trade-off he was willing to accept, especially in light of the close calls of the last couple of years.

Though, really, how close were those calls? Not very. Everyone knows that the police, especially the patrolmen on the streets, are extremely stupid. You could take one look at them and see what makes them tick. Teddy called it SDS: small dick syndrome. He'd never met a cop who didn't have the lethal combination of a tiny penis and an authority complex. They were so enamored with being tough, respected, and feared that they overlooked clear evidence or botched the scene with their own fingerprints and ineptitude. One cop in South Jersey—the one who'd almost crushed Teddy's windpipe while conducting a search for anything that might have belonged to little Amanda Kissel—had been so juiced up on steroids that he could barely walk. Teddy remembered the hilarious sound of the cop's polyester/nylon pants as his thighs rubbed against each other while he walked. It had been Teddy's simple comment—"Swish, swish"—that had almost gotten his windpipe broken.

Outsmarting the cops so consistently was ultimately the best revenge. Wasn't it sweet, poetic, and hilarious that little Teddy, who'd never weighed more than 115 pounds and who'd stopped growing when he hit 5'6", could mentally overpower, and thereby control, those gross ignorant law enforcers, who could lose their jobs if they stepped one inch out of line? The windpipe crusher had been suspended without pay indefinitely as Teddy's case made its way through the system. His lawyer—whom he'd hired to sue the cop, the police department, and the state of New Jersey—was trying for $30 million, but he'd told Teddy they could probably save a lot of time and aggravation by settling for $15 million. After the contingency fee was paid, that would leave Teddy with a cool $10 million or so. And it was a good thing, because he was running low on cash. He still got his disability and Social Security checks from the state, but a dollar didn't stretch very far these days. The money his mother had given him was long gone, used to pay for lawyers, his apartment, and a particularly greedy little man in the records hall whom Teddy paid handsomely to keep his name out of the national sex offenders registry.

A little extra money in the bank would indeed be welcome. Keeping up with technology was expensive, the price of high-speed connections going up all the time. And some of the magazines were extremely hard to get a hold of and required heavy outlays of cash. It wasn't uncommon to pay a thousand dollars for a single thirty-two page photo magazine.

Teddy got the magazines five or six times a year. He lived for those illicit meetings where money would change hands and the trade would be made. Sometimes he'd have to drive as far as North Carolina, or as far west as Ohio, to do the pickup. In the meantime, between issues, there was always the Web.

Yes, the Web, that miraculous invention. It made the days go by much more quickly. Of course, you had to be patient. Your schedule got messed up because the best people were online late at night, which meant you had to stay awake until the wee hours to get the best stuff, which meant you ended up going to bed at seven in the morning and sleeping until four or five in the afternoon. Some TV, maybe a frozen dinner or cup of soup, a shower, and then it was time to sign back on and wait for the carefully coded message that would begin a series of equally encrypted messages that would eventually lead to another precious magazine.

Dr. Cook, back at the institution, had warned him over and over that pornography was bad for him. It enflamed his desires, she said, and it managed to undo in fifteen minutes what he'd been fighting so hard for weeks or months. When the images were just in his head, he could make them disappear, but when he saw the actual pictures—that was when he did stupid things that hurt innocent children.

Dr. Cook didn't give herself enough credit, Teddy thought. He still hated her for what she'd done, for trying to keep him in the institution even though he'd been imprisoned there for fifteen years. But he *was* better than he'd been when Dr. Cook had first started counseling him. If he occasionally did something he wasn't supposed to do, it wasn't her fault. He was a human being. He made mistakes. Things happened.

Tonight he was watching his contacts list for CJ. CJ's Net name was "ChixJon," which his friends knew was short for "Chicken Jon." Chicken Jon was the mastermind behind three issues of Teddy's favorite magazine over the past two years. Teddy's conversations and correspondence with CJ had convinced Teddy that they were identical twins separated at birth. Both had the exact same tastes, the same erotic fantasies, the same sadistic streak, the same smooth tongue to charm the unsuspecting.

Teddy knew CJ wasn't a good influence on him. Two of CJ's magazines had caused him to go out and do stupid things, though his own brilliance combined with the stupidity of the police had prevented him from being arrested. CJ's last issue had appeared five months ago, on the day before Miguel Cruz had a fight with his stepfather and had run out of their apartment and into that park in Astoria, Queens. Miguel desperately wanted his own father back, not the mean and spiteful stepfather his mother had married. In a way, he was looking for a man like Teddy himself, who had a large apartment, lots of video games, and money to spend in arcades.

He'd vowed that Miguel would be the last one. For some reason, he'd been finding it harder to suppress the memories of Miguel's final pitiful moments than it was to suppress memories of the others. For the rest of his life, surfing the Net would have to suffice. Surfing, and those magazines from CJ and his associates.

He'd made a similar vow after Yolanda Harris, and again after Amanda Kissel. But this time he meant it.

CJ wasn't online today, but it was still early. That left Teddy enough time to run to the supermarket to pick up the caffeine and sugar he needed to get through another night on the Web. He'd drunk his last two cans of Pepsi yesterday, and his supply of Oreos, gummies, and Snickers was running low.

He quickly threw on a pair of sweatpants and a baseball cap. Five minutes later he was pulling his car out of the underground garage. He could have walked to the store, but he wanted to drive past the Mercedes dealership. As soon as the $10 mil came through, he was planning to ditch his old clunker Honda and trade up. Way, way up.

At the supermarket he loaded up on supplies to get him through the next couple of days: Cracker Jacks, pork rinds, fruit roll-ups, Mounds and Almond Joy, Reese's Pieces, Cadbury blocks, Pepsi, Mountain Dew, Orange Slice, Yodels, Twinkies, and Ho-Ho's. As he walked through the aisles throwing the junk food into his cart, he munched on a bag of Hydrox he'd opened in Aisle 3. A little old lady, watching him pull apart the bag and start chomping on the cookies like a madman, made a face of disapproval. *What's your problem, lady?* he wanted to say. *I'll pay for them at the register.*

He made his way to the checkout and threw his purchases on the belt. Off to the side were displays of individual candy bars. He picked up two Milky Ways, a Three Musketeers bar, two Butterfingers, and a Bounty and threw them onto the conveyor belt, too. The Bounty looked appetizing, so he unwrapped it and ate it as the cashier checked him out. The little old lady who'd been so disgusted when he wolfed down the Hydrox was behind him on the checkout line and made another face.

He used his debit card to pay for the $63 worth of junk. On his way out of the store, he reached into one of the bags and grabbed a Butterfinger. Juggling the bags, he ripped open the wrapping and shoved the entire bar into his mouth. He got chocolate and peanut butter all over the hatchback when he lifted it to place the groceries inside.

Back at the apartment, he threw his bags on the kitchen table and ran into the small bedroom. His pulse quickened when he saw that CJ was online and available to chat.

Hey CJ, he typed. *Did you have chicken for dinner?*

LOL was the response. *No chicken for dinner, too busy with my nature photography. What til you see what I have for you. I've outdone myself.*

D

C'est finis.

Sometimes in life, things just fall into place, as if the cosmos have aligned themselves into a preordained karmic syzygy. My own personal syzygy, as fate would have it, had a man on each end. On one end, John Althorp, Dean of Despair. On the other, Joseph Castro, a different kind of oppressor. Two men, each with a different name and appearance, a different profession, a different lifestyle. And yet in so many ways exactly the same man.

Geographically this worked out perfectly. "Big Joe," as some Manhattan ladies of the evening like to call him, lives/lived a mere twenty minutes from my apartment. Because Big Joe likes to make an impression when he enters or leaves a room, whether by bullying some smaller guy or leering at some young lady wearing a too-tight blouse, it was easy to observe him, both at a distance and up close. And that was perfect, too; certainly no man with that level of arrogance would think twice about an attractive woman checking him out.

A little research uncovered the fact that Big Joe isn't just a cop. He's a detective. That was a little sneaky of you, my fellow assassin, to leave that fact out. Perhaps you thought it would intimidate whoever got the assignment. But, you see, I do like a challenge. You don't navigate the shark-filled waters of academia your entire career and not learn how to bring down those who think they're much stronger and more powerful than you. And they do come crashing down, "with shuddering fall," as Joyce

Carol Oates might say, at which time they discover just how many people on whom they've trodden are celebrating their demise.

I knew better than to meet Big Joe for the first time on his own turf. His house was out of the question; only God knows how many guns and other weapons he had in there. Attempting to intercept him in his line of duty would have been suicidal, too; he would certainly have been armed. No, you have to get a man where's he weakest—in the groin—and when there's no firearm within reaching distance.

The research process had many benefits, not the least of which has been a renewed respect for my colleagues in the sociology department. In literary studies, much of what we do takes place within our own rarefied community of scholars and thinkers. We rarely encounter any "real people" as we search for details of what made Mary Ann Evans (George Eliot) tick or what Virginia Woolf meant in that particular passage in *Between the Acts*. So much time spent alone allows us to focus on our work and not be distracted by human frailties or insecurities. Not so when one is in the field, as it were, talking to living human beings with emotions, expectations, and experiences. How sociologists ever manage to get *any* research done and published is beyond me.

Since this whole arrangement is known only to you and me, I won't suggest to my friend X, a sociology professor specializing in social stratification, that she begin researching the gender-gone-wild phenomenon that is the club scene. But, mother of mercy, what a gold mine it would be. I'll never forget the evenings I spent at ■■■■■■■ Night Club. Those nights both opened my eyes and confirmed everything I'd long suspected about gender roles, the mating game, and a host of other topics not really relevant to my reason for going there.

It was easy to observe Big Joe the bouncer from various points within the club. One walks in to find Big Joe perched on a stool, wearing a short-sleeved shirt two sizes too small, the better to emphasize his bulging biceps. He's the essence of cool, wearing a gold chain, a man-bracelet, and slightly too much cologne. He checks the ID of each guy closely, the better to demonstrate his upper hand, his alpha-malehood, sizing up each twentysomething club kid to determine which of them he could beat up with one hand tied behind his back, and deciding smugly the answer is "all of them." With the ladies in tight minidresses he's Mr. Suave, flirting and telling them to "look for him later." With the ladies who are a bit overweight, or not as pretty as the others, he's just bored, checking the birth date on their drivers' licenses and then waving them in distractedly as he looks over their shoulders, down the line, for the next piece of fresh meat.

A few hours at ■■■■■■■ (during which I was treated to a never-ending onslaught of young men attempting to feed me Ecstasy as a way of getting me into bed) made it clear that Big Joe favored petite, dark-haired girls with big (or at least perky) breasts and who consider panties and brassieres optional at best. He also seemed to particularly enjoy chatting with women who'd arrived at the club with boyfriends or male friends. He isn't interested in talking with guys at all; I'd guess he doesn't have any male friends. One night he did chat with a tall, well-built guy for a few minutes. I was talking with the bartender and asked who the cute tall guy was. He said, "That's Nick, Joe's partner on the detective squad." I steered clear of Nick, who seemed just as predatory as Joe, the entire evening.

I have a sister who resembles me, and a cousin who does too. It was easy enough to borrow their ID's for a few evenings (without their knowledge, of course) so that Big Joe wouldn't get suspicious. Not that he'd particularly notice me, anyway, given the way I was (not) dressed and (not) made up. But, like Hamlet, I had a method to my madness. It was a waiting and observing game, so I waited and observed.

I closed the place three weekends in a row. Big Joe's M.O. never changed. Four of the six nights I was at the club, a young chippie (a different one each time) would separate from her group of scantily clad friends and begin hanging around the bouncer's stool. Once there, she was there to stay, until the club closed, at which time she went home with Big Joe. At least, that's what I'm assuming. Two nights I left early and parked near his house; both those nights he pulled up an hour later, followed by the young lady who'd been lucky enough to attract his attention.

One night Big Joe struck out. He'd had his eye on a blonde bombshell who'd cut him down to size once or twice. He'd given her a filthy look on her way out of the club. That night I decided to follow Big Joe if I could. That trip took me into the dingy West Side of Manhattan at 4 in the morning, where Big Joe visited some "bitches" who work the streets for a living. When I went back a few days later, posing as a journalist doing a story on why prostitution should be legalized, I heard tales of the cop who banged them, took their money, and got away with it time and time again.

In my quest for relevant information, I also asked the ladies about a drug I'd read about, the date rape drug Rohypnol. "Roofies," said one girl who looked like she'd been on the streets since she was born. "Bad shit, lady. Stay away from it." A bit more research convinced me I'd hit upon my weapon.

Now came the hard part. How did I get Big Joe to invite me back to his place? At first, I thought concocting a plan would require all my feminine wiles. But it required none of them. All I had to do was dress appropriately and make it clear that I wanted nothing more than to suck Joe Castro's cock and have him fuck me til I bled.

I will admit to mixed feelings as I went shopping for slut clothes and make-up. On the one hand, it was almost fun to see how the other half lived. You should have heard some of the conversations on which I eavesdropped while shopping at Mandee's and other stores that cater to, shall we say, girls who graduated high school with great difficulty. On the other hand, I hated myself for bringing myself down to this level, for cheapening myself just to get a man into bed.

Ultimately, though, I felt that the ends justified the means. Because this was to be a turnabout in its purest form. Men have the advantage of size and strength, especially men like Big Joe Castro. Women can't compete in those arenas, so we're forced to exploit our other advantages. Joe Castro clearly enjoyed taking advantage of women. Let's see how he liked it when a woman took advantage of him.

It took me a few hours of practice in front of a mirror in my apartment to perfect the look I wanted. For the purposes of this mission, and from that perspective only, I suppose I am fortunate: My breasts are round and ample, and all the running I've done has kept me lean and small-waisted. I can wear tight little dresses to show off my body, if I so choose, and I can apply make-up to emphasize what society would consider my best features. So that's exactly what I did.

My hair was going to be my Waterloo, though. I keep it short for many reasons, but mostly because I don't want the maintenance of long locks. But a wild mane of hair seemed to be a prerequisite for getting into bed with Big Joe. So off I went to a fairly upscale wig shop and came home with an expensive wig that transformed me. I didn't worry about Big Joe noticing it was a wig. Everyone knows straight men don't look too closely at anything besides breasts.

The last pieces of the costume were the ultra-high-heels I bought to complete the ensemble. The wig said "I want to blow you," and the dress said "I want you to fuck me." But it was those shoes that said "I'm a whore who'll do anything you want."

I've always believed that men are predictable and easily manipulated, and Big Joe's reaction when he saw me confirmed that I'd chosen the right method of executing my plot—and Joe. He looked me up and down, saying with a sparkle, "Haven't seen you before."

"My first time," I giggled girlishly.

"Got your ID?"

"Oh, no," I gasped, rummaging through my tiny club bag, as if not being allowed into the club would have caused the sky to come crashing down. "I must have left it in the car. I'll go get it."

"Nah, that's OK," Big Joe said. He looked/leered at me again and not-very-subtly flexed his bicep. I responded by thrusting my chest out slightly.

"Joe," he said, as if his name were the world's biggest aphrodisiac.

"Lana." It was as good a fake name as any. "Hey Joe, can I buy you a drink?"

"I'm the bouncer here...let me buy *you* a drink."

"Gladly," I giggled, then moved inside. The people waiting in line behind me were getting irritated at being delayed by the flirtation.

The entire evening I kept migrating back to Big Joe, who also left his perch occasionally to seek me out. I lamented that my two friends still hadn't shown up, as they'd promised. He responded by saying not to worry, he'd look out for me. I thanked him and moved slightly closer whenever his hand migrated to my hip or thigh. My hands did some migrating of their own as they explored his biceps and as I exclaimed with delight over their size and thickness. To my questions "How much do you lift?" and "How often do you work out?" I received long, detailed responses outlining his health and fitness regimen.

As I look back on it now, it was like being on stage for an evening. There I was, another person—"Lana." And I played my part exquisitely.

Closing time was looming. I had to tread carefully not to destroy everything I'd worked at the whole evening. I gave him a peck on the cheek about five minutes before last call and thanked him for being so nice and special. I said I'd been feeling lonely after being stood up by my friends but that the evening had been worthwhile because I'd met him.

"Yo, Lana, no way I'm lettin' you leave here by yourself. It's late. Hang out til the place closes and I'll walk you to your car."

I protested mildly but eventually agreed. We were the last two out of the place. The bartenders locked the doors behind us.

At my car Joe made his move. His lips came at me and I went with the moment.

"Oh," I sighed, affecting surprise. "That was nice, wasn't it."

"It was, Lana. I don't want this night to end. I still have lots of energy. You wanna come over to my place for some breakfast? I'm in Queens, about twenty minutes from here."

"I don't know, Joe...I'm tempted, but it's late..."

"Come on, it'll be fun. I'll be a gentleman. Unless you don't want me to be," he chuckled cockily.

"Ah," I responded flirtatiously, "If I like the gentleman so much, I'm sure I would also like the non-gentleman." God, it was so cornball and sickening, but it was working.

"Come on, follow me, we'll be there in no time."

"OK," I said, after a bit more protesting. "Let me just call my mother so she doesn't worry." That was a good touch, I thought. I pulled out my cell and called my own home phone, telling "Mom" I was going to a diner with the girls and I'd be home quite a bit later than I'd expected.

We were at Big Joe's house shortly thereafter. He drove slowly and carefully as I followed him. He wouldn't have wanted to drive too fast and lose his lay for the evening.

To my surprise, he really did want to cook breakfast. "How about some bacon and eggs?" he asked, after we'd kissed.

"I'll take two, over easy," I said. "And maybe a cup of coffee or a big glass of O.J.? I had a few drinks, and well, you know...."

"Of course," he said, pouring the two of us a tumbler of Tropicana each. "Hey, you don't mind if I change out of these smelly clothes? I wanna put a pair of sweats on."

"It's your house, Joe. Be comfortable. I wish I could get out of these clothes, too."

The look in his eye said: Never fear, you won't be wearing them too much longer.

As soon as he left the room I moved quickly. I removed the crushed-up roofies from my purse, dumped them into his orange juice, and used my finger to stir. I was sitting on the couch sipping my own O.J. when Joe came back wearing a short bathrobe over a pair of boxers.

I nodded approvingly, coyly, then raised my glass. "A toast. To friends not showing up."

He picked up his glass, and we clinked. Then we both chug-a-lugged.

As Joe cooked the bacon and eggs, he started to lose his balance a bit.

"Are you OK?" I asked, my voice reflecting a concern I didn't feel.

"Just sort of tired, a little dizzy maybe."

"Sit down, honey. Let me finish cooking. You just need some good food in you."

Joe made his way to the couch. In five minutes he was unconscious.

He really was a pig, lying there in his boxers like he was king of the studs about to give some poor dumb girl the fuck of her life. It made it that much easier to take the knife out of my purse and use it.

I know that A said not to use a knife because of the blood—and there was *a lot* of blood. But I couldn't get my hands on a gun, and I didn't know what else to use. I could have forced him to swallow more roofies, but I wasn't sure that would do the trick. So a knife it was: convenient, portable, easy to wield, and easily disposed of. And, I might add, quite satisfying.

I hadn't touched anything in the house except for the glass of orange juice, and I put that glass in my purse. I'd put on rubber gloves before stabbing him and had managed to jump out of the way before the blood started spurting heavily. I did get some blood on the dress, on the shoes, and on the wig, but all of those items would soon be disposed of. So, all things considered, I think I chose the proper weapon to get the job done.

I turned out the lights, locked the front door of the house, and returned to my car, which I'd parked down the block. On the way home, I pulled onto the side of the highway and pulled off the wig. I was home in less than half an hour. I took a nice, warm shower and scrubbed myself clean.

That was two hours ago now, and I think the adrenaline is finally wearing off. Writing everything down has calmed me down somewhat, so I think I'll turn into bed in a few minutes. Tomorrow I'll mail this letter and get rid of all the components of the "costume," first shredding them and then discarding them in various trash bins throughout the city.

This whole process has been liberating in the extreme. Through it, you and I have managed to rid the world of not one, but two, cancers. Thank you for the opportunity of a lifetime.

D

B

Hello:

When I received your letter with my assignment, I became extremely upset. I almost couldn't go through with my end of the bargain.

It wasn't because that animal didn't deserve to die. Quite the contrary. But as I read the letter, I came down with a horrible case of the shakes. It took me nearly two days to read it in its entirety. It was just too much too handle all at once. The stories of what your chosen had done and gotten away with, and the fact that he was living as a free man in a luxury apartment, hit at so many of my weaknesses. Including some weaknesses I hadn't even realized I had.

You don't know this, but I never married and never had any children. Not getting married was the right choice for me, and I have no regrets. But now that I'm alone and getting older, I find myself thinking about what it's going to be like to die by myself, to have my body found by nephew Nicholas on one of his rare visits, or by the meter reader or the man who mows my lawn. A child would have been a friend and companion in my old age. I couldn't even begin to imagine how those poor parents from Pennsylvania, New Jersey, and Queens must have felt after losing their children, who were supposed to have lived long lives and become their parents' friends and companions.

But that wasn't the only reason I felt sick and had to stop reading. I'll try to explain as best I can. I've always lived a sheltered life, and I've been happy that way. I've never been out of New York/New Jersey. Working full-time, taking care of Mother, and trying to maintain a home on a very limited income was always enough for me. I simply didn't have the energy or the money to do much else, and I never minded. All my life I did without many, many things, and here I sit today, healthy and fairly happy. So it's not like I needed *things* to give meaning to my life.

But the one thing, the one intangible, that's become increasingly important to me now that I'm older is *security*. By which I mean *safety*. I'm a woman alone. Lately I've become very aware that I can't protect myself against the horrors of the world, against muggers, rapists, thieves, drug dealers, and terrorists who destroy the World Trade Center. The reason I wanted to buy a house wasn't just to own my own home, though that was a big part of it. I also wanted to buy a house because I needed to get out of the Bronx, out of New York City.

If you're a younger person, you have no idea how things have changed in the last forty years. None of us had any money when I was a child, but the neighborhood was neat as a pin and we left our apartment doors unlocked. We played in the playgrounds, walked to and from school, and watched baseball games in Van Cortlandt Park. Our parents never worried about us. By the time I left the apartment in which I'd lived with my mother for more than sixty years, the entire neighborhood was filled with thieves and drug dealers. You couldn't go anywhere without a pack of people (safety in numbers), and you certainly couldn't go out after dark. Is that any way for people to live?

Moving to my suburban house was my way of trying to avoid the ugliness of the world. In a quiet house on a dead-end street you can hide away, especially if you don't watch TV news and don't read any newspapers. My home is my sanctuary. I don't want the world intruding on my four walls, and I've done a good job of making that happen. The appearance of a horrific new neighbor brought the world crashing down on my head, but I took steps to fix that situation.

And then I read my assignment, and the ugliness of the world, and of humanity, hit me in the face again. Reading it took me back to my old neighborhood, where children now end up dead before they reach adolescence and gang members blow rival gang members' heads off for fun. I hadn't thought about any of these things for years. But the letter forced me to think about them again.

And I realized something. Hiding behind my front door may help me protect myself, but it doesn't stop the world from getting worse. Maybe it was time for me, a slightly overweight, nondescript sixty-seven-year old lady, to do something to make the world a better place. A world more safe for children, and also for their parents.

You wouldn't believe the surges of adrenaline that my pursuit of Teddy gave me. Rather than simply going to work, coming home, and doing housework on the weekends, I had something to give my life direction and focus. It was *my* job—no one else's—to take care of this problem, to make sure no other children were kidnapped in Queens, Brooklyn, New Jersey, or anywhere else. I felt, and feel, energized. Renewed. Invigorated.

I've been familiar with only two neighborhoods in my almost seven decades—my old neighborhood in the Bronx, and now a few blocks in Bloomfield. But suddenly I was needing to travel all the way to Brooklyn. Never mind that it's only an hour's drive to Teddy's apartment from Bloomfield (without traffic). My assignment might as well have been in China.

Getting to and from Brooklyn via bus would have been doable, though extremely time consuming and awkward. A car was going to be necessary. The only problem was I'd never been behind the wheel of a car in my life.

He moved rapidly, keeping his head down. I followed at a discreet distance, just another old Brooklyn lady with white hair and a shopping bag.

His first stop was a deli a few blocks away. I put on my sunglasses and followed him inside. He bought sugary juice drinks, a copy of *The Clarion*, and a few candy bars, which he hungrily gobbled down as he was leaving the deli. I saw him turn the block to continue on what were probably a few more errands, but I felt I'd come close enough for one day. So I went back to my car and drove home to Bloomfield, feeling a sense of accomplishment.

The next day I was sitting on the same bench, wearing a different pair of sunglasses and an overcoat, when I saw his little Honda pull out of the garage, make a left, and come to a dead stop. Traffic was backed up about fifteen cars to the traffic light on the corner. I'd gotten a parking spot directly in front of the park, so I walked briskly to my car.

I followed him in my car as he drove to the supermarket. A few minutes after he entered, I did the same. I followed at a discreet distance while he loaded up the cart with junk food. I felt my skin crawl, and not because he was an ugly man to look at. On the contrary, some women his age would probably have found him cute despite the acne scars. You'd never know from looking at Teddy what he was capable of, which made him all the more dangerous. Which, in turn, made my mission all the more important.

As Teddy moved through the aisles, he kept shoving cookies into his mouth from a bag he'd opened. He was like a child who won't eat his dinner but then has a box of Mallomars for dessert, followed by a few popsicles and some ice cream. I wouldn't have been surprised if every tooth had rotted out of his head, but I didn't get close enough to see. His gluttony continued on the checkout line, where he practically swallowed an entire chocolate bar without chewing it.

After checking out, Teddy threw his grocery bags into the trunk of his car and sped away. So as not to seem suspicious, I stood in the front of the market checking my receipt. And then I headed home with some groceries I didn't really need.

I was pulling into my driveway when the idea hit me. A brilliant idea, actually. It couldn't have been more perfect. It would require a little finesse, and the right ingredients...but it couldn't fail. It was the perfect embodiment of that old saw, "Old age and treachery will easily overcome youth and strength."

There was just one part of my plan with which I wasn't 100% comfortable, but it was probably the most important part, the bait Teddy wouldn't be able to resist. After a bit more thought, I figured out how to pull it off.

My neighbor has an adorable ten-year-old daughter. I'll call her "Sara." Sara is a beautiful child who does well in school. She plays on the soccer team, and she's starting to take lessons on the clarinet. But Sara's favorite activity, bar none, is her Girl Scout troop. Every year for the past three years, she's sold more Girl Scout cookies than any other girl in Bloomfield.

A few days later, Sara and I made our way to Brooklyn in my trusty Buick. She looked adorable in her Girl Scout uniform, and she was excited at the prospect of expanding her territory, of using my out-of-state friends and relatives to sell more cookies. As we crossed the Goethals Bridge into Staten Island, I went over the rules: *Under no circumstances whatsoever was she to go into anyone's apartment.* Her mother had been telling her the same thing since she was a toddler, so Sara didn't need a lecture about it. Still, I didn't feel the point could be overemphasized.

Getting into the building could be a bit of a problem, as a doorman usually presided over the front entrance. But during my vigil, I'd seen the various doormen leave on a few separate occasions, once or twice to grab a smoke, a couple of times to help residents with their packages, and a few times to park tenants' cars in the garage. The doorman would abandon his post eventually, and we'd wait until he did.

Sara is a smart girl, and I was hard pressed to explain why we sat on the bench in the park outside the building for so long. I made up excuses, telling her that solicitors were allowed in the building only during certain hours, and that we needed to wait just a little bit longer. I promised her I'd buy a box of cookies for every fifteen minutes I made her wait, and that satisfied her. In the meantime, we played cat's cradle and I listened as she told me about her friends and school activities.

After we'd waited on that park bench for two hours, a car pulled up to the front door and an elderly man emerged from the driver's seat. The doorman got into the car and drove it down the hill into the garage. Sara and I were across the street, in the building, and in the elevator faster than you could say "Jack Sprat." The poor child. I almost pulled her arm out of its socket as we crossed ■■■■■■■■■ Street.

The car's owner got off on the sixth floor, and we continued to the twelfth. We rang a few doorbells. No one answered, of course; everyone was at work. When we got to Apartment 1210, I suggested to Sara that we'd sell more cookies if we split up. She agreed. I warned her once again *not to go into anyone's apartment under any circumstances, and to scream if she felt threatened or scared by anyone.* She looked at me as if to say, "Don't worry, it's under control." I patted her on the shoulder, took one of the order forms, and went around the 90-degree bend in the corridor, where I couldn't be seen. I waited there, listening as she rang each bell—Apartment 1211, 1212, 1213, 1214....

The door of Apartment 1215 opened.

"Hi," Sara said. "I'm with the Girl Scouts. We're selling cookies as a fund raiser. We have thin mints, and cheddar cheese crackers, and peanut butter goodies, and Samoas. Would you like to help support our organization by buying some cookies? They are only $4.50 per box, and all the money goes to a good cause."

I heard Teddy say, "Well, aren't you sweet. Let me see your cookie sheet."

Some paper rustled. He must have been looking at the color cookie brochure.

"Which are *your* favorites?" Teddy asked.

"I love them all, but definitely the thin mints." That Sara—she was an experienced saleswoman in a child's body.

"I think the Samoas are more my speed. I'll take four boxes."

"Thank you so much. Here's a pen. That will be eighteen dollars, please."

"I have to pay upfront? What a racket. OK, wait here, I'll get you the money."

Every second she spoke to him was like an hour. I silently thanked God that he'd asked her to wait in the hallway.

He returned a few seconds later. "When do I get the cookies?"

"We'll drop them off in about two weeks. Thank you so much for supporting the Girl Scouts."

"No, *thank you*," Teddy said. The door clicked shut.

I raced around the corner. Sara stood there, beaming.

"Sara, you're not going to believe this," I said. "The superintendent lives on the floor below us, and he wants to buy fifty boxes! But he says we have to leave the building now, because he's starting to get complaints."

"Oh, all right. Darn," Sara said. Clearly, she thought she could do a lot more damage than fifty boxes, but that was all my budget could handle.

"Come on," I said. "I'll make it up to you. Let's go have lunch. There's a deli around the corner."

When Sara went to use the lavatory at the deli, I slipped the order form out of her backpack. It was a new form with only Teddy's name and order on it.

She noticed the order form missing on the way home. "What could I have done with it?" she asked, upset.

"Don't worry about it, honey. I remember his apartment number. Do you remember what he ordered?"

"Yes, four boxes of Samoas."

"I'll just bring them to him when I bring the fifty boxes to the super." She was satisfied with this solution.

Back in New Jersey, I did a pre-emptive strike with her mother, telling her I'd miscalculated: My cousins hadn't been home and the super had been strict about not allowing solicitation in the building. She accepted the explanation and said 54 boxes wasn't bad, all things considered.

Those 54 boxes of cookies showed up at my house two weeks later. It was time for Step Two.

I took a trip to Hackensack, where a young woman in a medical supplies store sold me syringes for my "insulin injections." I then spent the rest of the day visiting various drugstores and supermarkets, always spending at least $25 in each one so the purchase of a single, possibly questionable item wouldn't stand out in their minds. Then again, who was likely to remember a chubby white-haired lady, anyway? But better safe than sorry.

The recipes A provided for fast-acting, lethal, odorless, tasteless poisons couldn't have been more useful. I concocted the one A called Potion 4. Then I used my hair dryer to loosen the glue on each of the four boxes of Samoas. The cookies were standing in individual slots on a plastic tray. The tray and cookies had been wrapped and sealed in a transparent film. I filled a syringe with the potion, then injected each cookie through the film. The syringe holes in the film were tiny, practically invisible to the naked eye.

I then used my glue gun to glue the box flaps back together. I wore surgical gloves during the entire procedure.

When I was done, I surveyed my work. The boxes looked pristine and untouched, as if they'd just come off the assembly line.

I went to Brooklyn for the last time the following day. This time I wore a hat and a different wig. I took my post on the bench. The doorman wasn't very cooperative; I waited nearly five hours for him to abandon his post. Then I was in the building, getting off on the twelfth floor, leaving the cookies suspended from the door of Apartment 1215 in a plastic Girl Scouts bag with a preprinted thank-you note, coolly taking the elevator back to the ground floor, getting into my car, and driving home.

All the way home I entertained myself with thoughts of that evil man ripping open the box of cookies and gorging himself, the way he'd done with the candy in the deli and grocery store. A's instructions said that even a small amount of the poison would cause death instantly. Which means those cookies could have killed a small army.

I tried not to think about several things. I wouldn't think about the way I'd used an innocent girl to further my plans, and I wouldn't think about what could have happened if he'd forced her into his apartment. (Everything I'd read about him had said he was cagey, not stupid, which meant he wouldn't have dared to try something as dangerous as that...but there had been a chance, no matter how small....) The building's lobby was monitored by a security camera, and I supposed we might be traced that way, though I'd taken great care to make sure that both my and Sara's backs were to the camera at all times. I also didn't want to think about what would happen if some unsuspecting person decided to nosh on a Samoa while collecting evidence at the crime scene. But there are rules against that, aren't there?

At this point, I can't tell you for sure that my plan worked. But I'd bet my house that it did.

I've had one or two minor guilt pangs. I never thought I was the kind of person who could do something like this. But I've done it. Now I just have to figure out how I'm going to spend the next twenty years. Maybe volunteer work? Maybe some vacations? Who knows? If this whole experience has taught me anything, it's that life is full of surprises.

Sincerely yours,

B

P.S. The traffic to and from my neighbor's house has been much lighter the last few days. I wonder if....?

A

From *The Clarion*

Investigators Looking for Connections in Two Murders
Deaths of Detective, Pedophile Linked?

The murder of Detective Joseph Castro last week sent shock waves through the Queens neighborhood in which he lived. Castro was found dead in his home last Monday by his partner on the detective squad, Nicholas Lang, who'd been concerned when Castro did not report for duty. Police say that Castro had been drugged with the date-rape drug Rohypnol, then stabbed to death.

The detective had been a highly respected and well liked member of the community, popular with both adults and children. In addition to coaching soccer and baseball, Detective Castro had been a mainstay of the NYPD's drug education program. In addition, he was under contract with Manor House to write a book about his experiences as a detective. His editor, Joan Ventre, said she had recently contracted for Detective Castro's as yet unwritten book, tentatively titled *The Everyday Killer*.

Detective Castro had been stationed in Astoria for the last five years and had been the lead investigator on a series of kidnapings. Colleagues say Castro was sure he'd found the man responsible for the disappearances but lacked sufficient evidence to make an arrest. *The Clarion* has learned that Castro's prime suspect was Jesse Garanowicz of ■■■■■■■■■■ Street in Brooklyn. Garanowicz, a convicted pedophile, had been living under the assumed name Teddy Boyle in Brooklyn after fleeing New Jersey, where he'd been under investigation for another series of child disappearances. One week before Detective Castro's death, Garanowicz was found dead in his apartment, the victim of poisoned cookies.

Police are investigating whether Detective Castro may have been involved in the murder of Garanowicz. Insiders say Castro's hatred of Garanowicz was well known in the force, and some speculate that Castro may have planned the execution of Garanowicz. However, at this time investigators have no evidence to prove that Castro was involved in the murder of Garanowicz, or that someone close to Garanowicz murdered Castro in an act of revenge.

"It's preposterous to think that Joe would arrange a murder," said Father Tomás Rodriguez of St. Elizabeth's R.C. Church, of which Castro had been a congregant his entire life. "Detective Castro was an upstanding citizen and an asset to our community. His death has been a terrible loss for us."

From the private journal of Father Tomás Rodriguez

Thank you, Lord, for this journal—for the relief it provides.

I cannot speak of my acts to anyone. Not even to Declan, my confessor. For to confess those acts is to go against every vow I have ever sworn, every promise I have ever made to you.

I thought I was obeying you, Heavenly Father.—But was it your dark rival who convinced me I was doing your work? Is it not your decision whom to punish, and when? What right had I to make that decision?

But I could not let him get away with it. I could not allow a killer to continue his game, the conscription of others into his evil circle of murder. For is not the conscription of others into mortal sin, the greatest, most unforgivable sin of all?

Heavenly Father, I misused the trust placed in me. I acted on what I heard in my capacity as counselor and confessor to sign a man's death sentence. I used the confession booth as an interrogation chamber, to discover that a man who lived an outwardly upstanding and moral life was plotting the deaths of five people—one of his own choosing, and four chosen by those unknown to, but managed by, him.

Did I do your work too assiduously, Father? Did I usurp the roles of judge, jury, and executioner?

I ask myself these questions daily. And I pray. I pray for Dr. John Althorp, who will never know how lucky he is to be alive. I pray for myself and the families of the victims and the victims themselves.

For now the detective, the man who called himself "A," is dead. The Circle of Assassins has come full circle.

Part 4

Maria Lentricchia

Dear Rossella:

I cried for hours after I read your letter. Please understand, I don't mean to ignore you. I hate that we've grown apart like this. Remember in high school? We vowed "best friends forever." And then you move to California, & my life gets busy with work & the wedding & everything else, & before you know it way too much time has passed.

I appreciate you offering to come out for a visit. YES, I want you to come. But not now. Maybe next month or a couple of months from now? I will call you back soon, I promise—I just can't now. I can't talk to anyone without breaking apart and I'm tired of being such a mess all the time. The doctor gave me some pills, they are helping. They calm me down and help me sleep, but what I need is a pill that stops me from crying, so that I won't have a headache all day long. Maybe in a few more weeks I'll be able to hold myself together long enough to have a normal human conversation.

This is why I'm doing email. My voice cracks when I try to talk & my hands shake when I try to hold a pen. At least with a keyboard I can get the words down. And as I sit here typing this I think to myself, we have had each others' email addresses all along, why don't we email more often? Why am I so bad about keeping in touch? The answer isn't because we're not still best friends. It's because I'm selfish and I don't make the time. And I'm sorry, Rosie, I am so sorry.

Before what happened to Rog, me and my mother were having a fight about what else, the wedding, and she said all brides are selfish and I was no exception. And I think she was right. To be honest with you I was selfish then & I am feeling selfish now, too. Not because my wedding day was stolen from me, who CARES about some stupid wedding, but because the man I love was stolen from me, for a couple hundred bucks in his wallet. And you know what the worst part is, the part that makes me shake when I think about it? Rog never used to carry a lot of money around with him, it was only in the last few months he started doing that. And I know why, he wanted my father to think he deserved me. You know my father, he has that effect on people, somehow he always makes them feel like they'll never be as successful as he is. So some dirtbag at the Lido (yes it's still there & still full of lowlifes) sees Rog flashing his wallet, sees the cash, follows him out to the truck, & that's that. The end of Rog's life and the end of mine too.

I've been praying to be a better person but I can't get away from this selfishness. In life I had to share Roger and it's still that way, I have to share him with his family, his friends, the guys he works with, his ex-girlfriends who keep calling me to say how great he was, even my own family too. Everyone loved him & they are trying to be there for me, but I have to be there for them too. And I don't want to be. I want it to be all about me, about everyone feeling sorry FOR ME because I was the most important person in his life, not them. I don't want to waste the tiny amount of energy I have left to make someone else feel better. I want to use it to make myself feel better, but other people need me & they refuse to stop needing me even though they don't know that's what they are doing. The pain is too unbearable for everyone & everyone thinks her pain is the worst.

Rog's mom won't talk to me. She flipped out on me at the funeral, Rog's dad had to hold her back. Meanwhile my dad had to hold me back. When Rog's mom started coming at me, I went at her, I didn't know whether I was going to hug her tight or punch her face. Because we always got along but she used to make comments that never sat right with me, like "Oh Maria, I hope you don't mind chicken, we can't afford all the fancy meals your mother cooks when we go to her house" & "How is your sister doing with her diet? She would be such a pretty girl if she could lose some of that weight" & "Maria, I don't want to tell you how to plan your wedding but if I were you..." & "I'm sorry I keep calling you Gabrielle, it's just that Rog was with her for so long and we were so close."

And we probably will never talk again because the funeral was the last time we saw each other. I know she blames me for what happened, she was screaming about how terrible my family is, how we tried to change Rog, and other horrible things I can't write here because I have tried so hard to forget them, I can't even remember them now.

Even MY mom & dad are upset beyond words, my mother was the bigger person, she stood there & took it & didn't say a word when Rog's mom was screaming all those insults at us. My folks truly loved Rog as a son even if he did aggravate them once in a while. That's how my father knew he was one of the family already, he said he used to get as mad at Rog as he gets at his own kids, & he doesn't have that sort of feeling for anyone outside the family.

I don't know what's harder to think about, the good times or the fights. He could be such a pain in the ass about his sports & his buddies & those stupid things they used to do, like those asinine Super Bowl parties & those filthy bachelor parties, all the girls know each stag party got raunchier & raunchier as they tried to outdo each other in grossness. At the beginning that stuff didn't bother me but my mom & my sister (& sometimes my dad) were always in my face about it, I don't know how they found out about that stuff but it seemed like they always did. And they'd get me worked up & then I'd be all uptight around

Rog & we would end up fighting over something that in my heart I really didn't care about. And sometimes just before the pills kick in those fights get replayed in my head on an endless loop & I just want to claw my own eyes out or scream at all of them for putting idiotic ideas in my head that didn't matter because MY relationship was between ME & ROG, not them, & why were they always butting their fucking noses into MY business with the man who was going to be MY husband.

And I think all the bad thoughts swirling around in my head are not just guilt for getting on Rog's case but also because I am trying so hard not to think about something, about a conversation me & him had a couple of months ago where he was carrying on & being a jerk, & I was being a bitch back at him, & he actually sounded worried about something & I didn't want to hear it because we were going out for a fancy dinner in the City & I didn't want the night ruined from him getting all dramatic about my brother over some stupid high school rivalry they never ironed out. Rosie you must NEVER EVER tell another person what I am writing to you, which is that Rog was afraid Leo might kill him. At the time I thought I never heard anything so ridiculous in my life, Leo's not that smart but he's harmless, & I didn't get all the details from Rog, something about a fight in the parking lot of a diner & a threat, but it was all so stupid & just more of the same idiotic bullshit. The two of them were always at each other's throats, I don't know why, they never liked each other & I kept hoping the situation would get better but it never did. I thought Rog should be the bigger man, he is smarter than Leo & has so many more friends, why couldn't he just include Leo more in activities with his buddies & be a little nicer to him? And Leo was right, Roger was disrespectful to me & my family sometimes (though he didn't really mean to be, he just didn't think a lot of the time), how could I get mad at my brother for basically sticking up for me? That's what brothers are supposed to do. I'm sure if Tony was still living in NYC he would have felt the same way, but since he got married & moved upstate he has his own life, & Leo is really the only brother I have who is still around.

The police checked everything, they heard from Rog's friends that Leo didn't like him, so they came to the house to talk to my brother. But Leo was out in the City with three of his friends the night it happened, he was nowhere near the place Rog was, there are dozens of people who saw Leo & everything. So they let Leo go, but that didn't help around my house, when everyone is barely holding it together anyway. One of Rog's friends told the cops Leo didn't show any emotion at the funeral, which is true, but does that mean he killed Roger? Leo isn't an emotional guy, he holds everything in, just because he wasn't crying didn't mean he wasn't feeling awful & horrible like the rest of us.

One night I flipped out screaming & yelling I wanted everyone to leave me alone, to stop handling me with kid gloves & treating me like a baby instead of a grown woman. So everyone went out to dinner so I could have the house to myself to just mope around or break things or do whatever I wanted to do without having PEOPLE around me on my ass every second of the day, like they are afraid I'm going to kill myself or something. And yes of course I have thought about it, wouldn't you?—but not for very long, it's more of a passing thought but don't worry Rosie, I am going to get through this & there is nothing to worry about.

When the car pulled out of the driveway & I was sure they were gone, I snuck into Leo's room. I had to prove to myself in my own mind he was innocent so I could stop thinking about it. And I hunted around in the mess & I found the usual guy things, porn & rubbers & hair gel, & some textbooks on his computer desk, & underneath a paving brick paperweight printouts of emails from a girl he has been flirting with on the Internet, who sounds pretty dumb from the way she writes.

But then I made a mistake, I looked under his bed. Leo was never much of a reader but I found a bunch of paperbacks under there, books about unsolved murders & true crime stuff about serial killers like Ted Bundy & the Boston Strangler & a couple of issues of some gun magazines & a magazine called Soldier of Fortune which I never heard of but which has some really sick shit in it. And in a plastic bag under the bed there was a Mr. Clean cap, part of a costume or something, to cover your hair & make you look like you are bald. Leo never dresses up for Halloween, why would he have something like that under his bed? I thought it might be some kind of sex toy, like those toys that guys without girlfriends buy, but it was definitely a bald wig, the original packaging was in the bag.

And I went back to my room & I sat there very quietly until everyone got home, & when my mother went to bed I went down to the basement where my father hangs out & I told him everything. I said I thought Leo might have something to do with Rog dying, how Rog was afraid of Leo, & I told him about the stuff I found in Leo's bedroom. He just listened & didn't say anything until I was done & then he said, "You won't speak of this to anyone, Maria. I'll take care of everything."

And so a few days later when everyone was out of the house again I sneaked back into Leo's room & looked around again, & everything on the desk & dresser was gone, & so was everything from under the bed. And two days later the furniture company comes and delivers all new furniture for my brother, & my father & brother take the old stuff out to the backyard and through the window I watch them chop everything up with axes and then put everything into a fire & burn it, just like when the old Italians burn their leaves in the fall.

I tell myself it should be over, I need to work on healing myself & maybe helping Rog's mom heal too, & I should put everything behind me & not think about Leo & what he might have done, even though he could not have done what I think he did because all his friends (and various strangers, bartenders, etc.) <u>say they saw Rog at that bar in the Village the night Rog got killed</u>. I think about calling the cops & telling them what I found & what I think but how can I do that? How can I wreck my family the way Rog's family is wrecked? I can't put my mother through what Rog's Mom is going through, I can't narc on someone in my own family. My father would never forgive me, neither would anyone else, & I already feel alone enough as it is. And what if I am wrong? I found just a few stupid things that didn't make sense but we all have private lives the rest of the world doesn't know about, I have a few skeletons in my closet too (& you know what some of them are, just the way I know some of yours, but there are things I'm sure I don't know about you & things you don't know about me, because we all have to keep parts of ourselves for ourselves only). So what if my brother likes to read murder books, so do a lot of other people, the best seller lists are all about violence & mysteries. And what's the big deal about the bald cap, maybe it was a prank or something on a buddy of his, who knows?

One thing is for sure, I will never know & I have to learn to live with that. And with the guilt of not listening to Rog when he told me something was wrong.

Rosie we don't say these things often enough in life but I love you like a sister & I want us never to go this long without talking again. I will call you as soon as I am ready, I promise.

Love,
Maria

Leo Lentricchia

Transamerica Communications
Human Resources Department
1355 Broadway • New York, NY 10036

Mr. Leo Lentricchia
4271 ■■■■■■■■■■ Avenue
Throgs Neck, NY 10465

Dear Mr. Lentricchia:

Per our phone conversation, I am enclosing the documents you will need to complete prior to beginning employment with Transamerica Communications on the first of the month. Please fill out all the forms in this package and return the white and yellow copies to me. Retain the pink copies for your records.

We are delighted to welcome you to the Transamerica family. You will be working on Crew J178 based in Wakefield. Your immediate supervisor will be Trevor Wambelo, who will meet you here in my office two weeks after your start date, after you've completed your orientation and training.

As you know, the competition for our entry-level positions is quite intense. We had many excellent candidates, but we were impressed by your level of commitment and your enthusiasm for the work. Ultimately, though, we were most influenced by the glowing recommendations you received from Roger Borelli, Jack Mestre, John Harillo, and the other members of Crew J178.

We all look forward to having you on board.

Sincerely,

Cassandra Wells
Associate Director of Human Resources

Well, it was time to start learning. I enrolled in driving school. The young man who instructed me told me I was much more composed than the other "old people" he'd taught to drive. My eyesight is still decent, and my reflexes are still good, so I passed the road test easily. I used my small savings to buy a used Buick, which is roomy and comfortable. And before I knew it, I was driving back and forth to Brooklyn.

I'm not going to say that driving on the New Jersey and New York highways isn't nerve-wracking. Have you ever driven on N.J. Route 3, or gone across the Verrazano Bridge at rush hour? Ever try to finesse the bizarre curves and deadly potholes of the Belt Parkway? If you can avoid those routes, as I did for so long, please do. But my mission meant that I had to brave all those roads, and more.

You know what the funniest part of all of this is? I went without a car for 67 years and never felt deprived. Now, if you tried to take my Buick away, I'd fight you to the death for it.

For the first time in 30 years, I took time off work. My boss was so alarmed that he asked me if I was having a health scare. I just laughed and said a distant cousin was visiting from California and that I wanted to spend some time with her. He looked relieved. Relieved I was feeling fine, and relieved that the best secretary he'd ever had wasn't going anywhere.

During the research phase, I'd read up on the story of Jesse Garanowicz from Pennsylvania, now Teddy Boyle living in Brooklyn. The news stories only strengthened my determination and increased my resolve. The pictures included with the letter were very helpful. I committed Teddy's looks to memory, then made my way to Brooklyn for closer observation.

Teddy's building sits across the street from a park. I sat in the park for two days before I saw him emerge from the front door and cross the street. He was shockingly small and skinny.

Nick Lang

Walking through the front door of his former partner's house in Astoria, Queens, Nicholas Lang felt...what? He wasn't sure he had the right word in his vocabulary, or that such a word even existed. Not emptiness—no. Not numbness. Something else.

A month earlier, Joe hadn't reported for duty. Trying to determine his very reliable partner's whereabouts, Nick had driven to Joe's house with a mild sense of foreboding. He'd peeked in the front window to see Joe lying in a pool of blood on the living room floor, and he'd used the key hidden in the backyard to enter the house through the back door. Once in the living room, he'd made it onto the front porch in just enough time to prevent himself from vomiting on, and destroying possible evidence at, the crime scene.

His supervisor had ordered him to go home for the night, but he'd disobeyed orders and returned to the house an hour later to find an archetypical TV murder site. Tape on the living room floor marked where Nick had found the body. Cops and the guys from the M.E.'s office were milling around, doing their usual things but without the usual wisecracks. Flashes of light came through the curtains from photographers' cameras outside, as did snippets of the nonsensical yammering of reporters with perfect hair and monstrous egos talking into microphones about the tragedy, the shock, the horror of it all.

Now the living room looked almost as if his partner hadn't been stabbed to death in it. The bloodstains had been more or less scrubbed out of the carpet, and the couch, which had soaked up Joe's blood like a sponge, was gone. But that ugly lamp still stood in the corner, and the flat screen TV for which Joe had paid top dollar still hung on the wall. Nick wondered what would happen to that TV. Sharon or Eileen probably wouldn't want a reminder of their dead ex-husband hanging on the wall of their TV rooms. Maybe he could offer to buy it before they sold it to someone else. Most likely when he made the offer, they'd just give it to him.

Nick felt no guilt about plotting to acquire his dead partner's television. You couldn't work among criminals, and see hate at work every day, and then go home and romanticize emotions and relationships. The facts of the case were simple: Joe had been his partner. Joe had been murdered. A top-of-the-line TV needed to be disposed of. Either Sharon and Eileen could sell it for some ridiculously low amount to a stranger, or they could give it to the dead man's partner, who deserved it much more.

So, no, he wasn't about to feel guilty for trying to snag an expensive electronic toy. There was much more to feel guilty about. Like the fact that he and Joe weren't as close as a lot of other partners. And the fact that he had never really liked Joe. It wasn't as if he were *happy* that his partner had been murdered. On the contrary, he was almost blinded by his anger. But his anger was directed not at his partner's death but rather at the murderess and her audacity. How could such an intelligent woman not have understood that no detective in New York City would rest a single minute until she'd been found?

And it hadn't been that difficult to find her. Joe's love of gadgets had helped his colleagues considerably in that regard. Like many security-conscious professionals, he'd installed hidden cameras in his home—at the front door, in the living room, in the basement, and in the master bedroom. (Nick didn't want to think about the other possible uses for the bedroom camera.) And there all of it was, on tape. Joe and the whore at the

171

front door, all lovey-dovey and hanging on each other, both ready and willing to make the other into the evening's sexual conquest...Joe going into the bedroom to change from bouncer gear into something more comfortable...the woman slipping something into his orange juice...Joe conking out...and the crazy bitch hacking at his unconscious body as if she wished she could cut him into a million small pieces and flush them down the toilet.

She'd calmly left the house, locking the door behind her, before moving out of the camera's range. She dripped tiny droplets of blood on her way back to her car, which had been parked a block away in front of the home of a perpetual insomniac. Old Mr. Dougherty had been watching TV in his living room at the front of his house when he heard the jingle jangle of car keys. He saw a long-haired woman get into a 2002 Toyota Corolla (Mr. Dougherty knew his cars) and drive away. He thought the first few letters of the license plate were RHP. A DMV search located two Toyota Corollas beginning with that sequence of letters whose owners lived within a fifty-mile range of Joe's house. EZ Pass records indicated that one of those Corollas had driven across the Triboro Bridge about 20 minutes after the estimated time of Joe's death.

They arrested Annette Bain approximately 24 hours after Joe died. She'd refused to speak to them without an attorney, of course. But the late Johnnie Cochran himself wouldn't have been able to get Annette Bain off. As the tapes showed, she'd put on gloves before killing Joe, but on her way into the house she'd made the mistake of touching the doorknob. They had two excellent fingerprints that exactly matched hers, as well as tiny drops of Joe's blood that they'd collected from under her fingernails. For now she sat in a holding pen, awaiting the next steps in a process that would land her in prison for the rest of her life. But she needn't worry about growing old in prison;

Nick was sure she wouldn't last more than a year. There were ways to make things happen in prison, carefully staged accidents and fights that could easily get a frail woman killed. In the meantime, the tabloids were having a field day covering every facet of the life of the controversial Mendham College English professor accused of a brutal premeditated murder.

He'd watched from behind the two-way glass as Tseng and Morrison grilled her. She'd sat there stone-faced, not saying a word, her arms folded. Occasionally she pursed her lips; sometimes her eyes flared. But never a word from Annette Bain. Tseng had ended his interrogation by asking calmly, quietly, "Why? Why, Miss Bain? Why would you do this to a New York City detective?" And still the suspect refused to speak.

"Why?" was the big question, of course. Was Annette Bain one of Joe's many ex-girlfriends or one-night stands come back for revenge? She wasn't Joe's usual type, that was for sure. Too intelligent and too independent. But you never knew with Joe....

In the meantime, they couldn't rule out the possibility that she was a psychopath/serial killer and that Joe was one of her random victims. They were running records, checking reports, looking for a pattern of similar murders in the tri-state area over the last five years, but they were coming up blank. Nick wasn't surprised. Everyone knows there's no such thing as a female serial killer. It had to be personal. Very personal.

Against orders and procedure, he'd paid a visit to Mendham College in plain clothes and engaged some students, faculty, and staff in conversation. Everyone was talking about Dr. Bain, and in his short visit Nick discovered an intensely divided campus. Friends and colleagues swore that Annette Bain, a serious scholar and literary theorist, simply wasn't capable of such savagery. Detractors and enemies had no trouble believing that a woman as intense as Dr. Bain would have no trouble slicing a man apart.

"Shit, she threw me looks like she wanted to kill *me*," said a burly football player wearing a T-shirt that read YOUR RETARDED. "Total man hater."

It made sense that a woman like Annette Bain would find a man like Joe repellent, Nick thought. Joe was a hard guy to like and an easy guy to hate. Even the women who once loved him ended up loathing him. When you looked at Joe as a whole, his positive qualities were never quite strong enough to outweigh the bad. He was a great detective: brave, hard working, committed to justice, aware of and protective of his role as a New York City "hero" after 9/11. He was a terrific and beloved coach; two of the girls from his soccer team had fainted at his funeral. His neighbors had loved having him in the neighborhood; everyone in New York City knows that an area is safest when cops and/or the Mafia live there. But at the end of the day, Joe Castro was a brute and a bully. An egomaniac on a power trip. A puppet master who loved nothing more than pulling the strings from behind the scenes.

Did Nick trust Joe with his life? Yes. Did he enjoy Joe's company and want to hang out with him on their days off? Absolutely not, though he occasionally did so.

* * *

Eileen and Sharon were sitting in the kitchen, drinking coffee and chewing on what looked like a week-old Entenmann's crumb cake. The two women couldn't be more different, but somehow they'd managed to bond, even before Joe's death. Both were in the position of knowing what it had been like to marry and live with Joe Castro, and their friendship had deepened over the years.

Two weeks before his death, Joe had changed his will to leave everything to his ex-wives, a fact that would have made them suspects if a videotape hadn't clearly shown Annette Bain committing the murder. Sharon and Eileen had agreed to sell the house and all its contents, then split the money 50/50. The realtor had suggested they wait a few months to put the house on the market, as no one would want to buy a place in which a man had been recently murdered, and some unscrupulous types might attempt to use the tragedy to negotiate the price. But people have short memories, the realtor had promised, and a few months down the road, after new carpeting had been installed and the place had been freshly painted, they'd get top dollar. In the meantime, though, the two women were selling off Joe's worldly goods little by little: the dining room set to a family who'd just moved to the neighborhood from India, the stereo to a teenager who lived next door, the DVD collection to the video rental store a few blocks away.

Nick gave each of the women a hug and a peck on the cheek. He liked both of them, but in different ways. Sharon had always been strong and outspoken. He liked that quality quite a bit in women he considered friends, less so in women he considered girlfriends. Eileen was warmer, more touchy-feely, but definitely the higher maintenance of the two. It was no surprise that neither one's marriage to Joe had worked.

"Thanks for coming, Nick," Eileen said as Nick took a seat at the table with them and ripped off a piece of the coffee cake with his fingers.

Nick nodded. "Looks like you've gotten rid of a lot stuff."

"Any news?" Sharon asked.

"No. She hasn't said a word, and she won't say a word until the verdict is read. Maybe not even then. Her lawyer's good. She won't let her say anything, and Annette Bain is smart enough to listen to a good lawyer."

"When I think of how many times I said I wanted to kill him...." Eileen began. "People throw that word around, don't they? 'Kill.' How many times a day do we say it? But no one ever thinks about what it means."

Nick thought, *I think about it all the time. But I'm a detective, it's my job to think about it. Believe me, you're better off not thinking about it. You're better off not spending your time around people who do it.*

Sharon nodded slowly. "Nick, we asked you to come for a reason. Joe left something for you."

"What is it?"

"We don't know, Nick. It's up in the attic, to the right of the window. We found it when we were cleaning up there."

Nick rose from the table and climbed the stairs to the second floor, then opened a small door containing a narrow staircase to the attic room Joe used as an office. He'd been in the attic only once before, when he'd helped Joe carry a heavy bookcase up the stairs.

Nick flipped on the light switch at the foot of the staircase and began slowly climbing the stairs, feeling the temperature rise with each step. At the top of the staircase, he surveyed the room. Joe was remarkably tidy. The room was filled with books, papers, sporting trophies, magazines, and storage crates, but everything was neatly organized.

He walked to the attic's single window opposite the staircase. To the right of the window he saw a large chunk of metal—an old filing cabinet. Each of the cabinet five drawers was labeled: A, B, C, D, and E. Taped to the front of the cabinet was a large envelope with the words

NICK LANG

written on it in Joe's handwriting.

Nick tried opening the cabinet. It was locked.

He loosened the tape surrounding the envelope and pulled it off the cabinet, then sat down on Joe's desk chair. Using an envelope knife he found on the desk, Nick sliced open the envelope and shook out the contents: a note and two keys.

Nick:

You have two choices.

(1) Find a way to get rid of this filing cabinet without opening it. Haul it out of here, take it to the dump, and have it crushed while you watch.

(2) Open it and read through everything. Start with the drawer marked A, then read B, C, D, and E. When you're done reading, decide what has to be done. Before you start reading, though, go to the U.S. Mail Stop on ■■th Street and retrieve the last pieces of the puzzle from box 175.

I hope she didn't make too big a mess of me.

Joe.

Annette Bain

Marcia—

How do you do it? How do you deal with the dregs of humanity on a daily basis? From everything I've been reading (and there's plenty of time to read, for once in my life), solitary confinement is supposed to be the worst sort of torture. Somehow the "experts" think that depriving prisoners of human contact is an effective method of punishment. But let me tell you this: If good behavior weren't so essential to my appeal, I'd be making all sorts of trouble just to get tossed into a pen far from everyone else.

The conditions are subhuman, the food awful, the stench unbelievable. But the worst part of being in prison is living with these depressed, filthy women who haven't had one abstract thought in their entire lives. Every last one of them is here for the same reason: a man, or men. Who got caught hiding drugs for her boyfriend. Who got tired of being slapped around and blew the asshole's brains out. Who helped her husband embezzle money, then got sold down the river when he took a plea deal. And the biggest irony is that so many of them look like exactly like the guys you'd see at biker bars, ogling strippers and then raping them on the pool table. Some of the ladies on my cell block have biceps so huge they could take down the world arm wrestling champion.

I'm starting to think I went into the wrong discipline. Within my first week in this pit I learned it's impossible to talk about literature or, for that matter, anything related to higher learning. (The library is filled with a surprising number of good books that nobody reads, while fist fights break out over who gets the only copy of the latest James Patterson book.) But the inmates *are* willing to talk about themselves and their problems endlessly. If I'd gone into sociology instead of literary studies, I would have been better trained in field research, in which you're forced to spend huge amounts of time among the people you're studying. Still, I've started to take notes for a book that I'll write when I've gotten out of here. I know you're working on that, Marcia, but please—work harder. If you were able to get Jean Merinetti off, you can get me off, too. My innocence is an added bonus that should make your job easier.

I've had to walk on eggshells to make sure I don't offend those in charge—a situation not unlike a college campus, where people much less intelligent than you end up with a disproportionate amount of power to make your life miserable. I seem to have fallen afoul of Merydith, a bull dyke security guard who was inexplicably offended by my support of her queer lifestyle. Big Kim, a lifer who killed her two kids so her boyfriend wouldn't leave her, also loathes me. Like most provosts and deans of students, she's borderline retarded and threatened by any show of intelligence. She doesn't understand half of what I say because her vocabulary is so limited, and she chooses to be offended by the mere fact that I use polysyllabic words. I've learned to steer clear of her. Her kind of stupidity, combined with her general level of malice, is a deadly combination.

So I keep my mouth shut, for the most part. Everyone likes the person who listens more than she speaks, and since the women here love nothing more than someone who will listen to them, I've found a small group who've taken a liking to me. They save a seat for me at mealtimes and give me tips on how to get by. I also get the sense that they quite approve of the crime of which I'm accused. I'm in my mid thirties, and I can say honestly that prior to this extremely unfortunate set of circumstances, I've had very few dealings with the police. But most of the women in here have had negative experiences with cops almost from the minute they were born. It's always the same story: fat, ugly guys compensating for their many inadequacies by becoming police officers and then using the law to make others feel small and powerless. These ladies have seen their drunken mothers cracked over the head with billy clubs; they've been pulled over for speeding and told the ticket would be ripped up in exchange for a complimentary blowjob; they've called the cops when their husbands were beating them and heard the yawns of boredom in the background because it was just too much effort for the police to haul their fat asses out to the trailer court *again* to deal with the problems of some bitch who probably deserved a good smack anyway. So the fact that I'm accused of quite viciously murdering a cop/detective gives them a surprising amount of respect for me. "You've got a set of balls," a woman named Andi said to me admiringly. "You did something everyone only *thinks* about doing." Welcome to America—the nation that hires thousands of men with obvious psychological and social problems to protect the citizenry.

I suppose I should be thankful for these new pals, as pretty much everyone else has abandoned me. I've tried writing to friends from grad school, and to colleagues with whom I thought I'd bonded at various conventions, but the responses have been few and brief. Even my old officemate at Mendham, Gretel Liebtrau, seems to have written me off. You haven't abandoned me—at least not yet, while I still have the money to pay you. I'd thought that getting tenure would have at least kept me out of the poor house, but just yesterday I received a carefully worded letter that the administration has begun proceedings to revoke my tenure on the grounds of "moral turpitude." Turpitude—does anyone outside academia use that ridiculous term? The process will probably take about six months, during which time

I'll continue to draw my salary as if I'm on sabbatical, but then that's the end of it. And when there's no money left, where will you go? My case is so high profile...you'll be set for life when (I won't say *if*) our appeal succeeds. You'll finally achieve true Celebrity Attorney status thanks to me, so I'm hoping that gives you some incentive (beyond money) to stick around.

Since I'll be bankrupt soon anyway, I wanted to ask you: Do you also take on litigation work? I'm thinking about suing the *Journal of Victorian Studies.* With nothing to do in here, I used my first three months to finish the article I'd been working on for nearly a year. It's quite possibly the best piece I've ever written, and I sent it off with great confidence. The editor-in-chief, *who actually served on my dissertation committee*, knew the topic and had more or less assured me at last year's MLA meeting that the article would be accepted for publication immediately upon receipt. But months passed and I heard nothing...until about two weeks ago, when I received a form rejection letter stating that it hadn't passed muster with the readers. It's pretty obvious what's going on, isn't it? I'm being discriminated against because of my status as an accused criminal (I *refuse* to use the term *convicted felon* until our last appeal fails).

So I'm thinking a lawsuit might be just the shock the *JVS* editorial board needs. I built my career by not letting anyone push me around, and I'm not about to become a shrinking violet just because I'm rotting away in prison. Literary journals have no money whatsoever; defending a lawsuit like this will absolutely bankrupt them. The audacity! The sheer hypocrisy! A university-sponsored research journal, whose stated goal is the furtherance of scholarship, *actively discriminating* against a well-regarded scholar whose innocence has not yet been finally proven! Just thinking about it makes my blood boil. In the meantime, I've submitted the article under a pseudonym to *Victoriana*, a rival journal. When it's accepted for publication there—as it no doubt will be—we'll have an even stronger case against *JVS*.

In the meantime, I can't let my emotions get the better of me. Losing control won't accomplish anything. And believe me, when I'm finally out of here, I *will* have the career I deserve to have, the one that's been interrupted by this bizarre accusation of murder. The world's full of stories of convicted felons who went on to greater success and contentment when their prison terms were up. Look at Martha Stewart (too strong and successful in her own right; had to be taught a lesson)—she's wealthier and more popular than she's ever been, probably because the public realized how intensely she'd been railroaded. I never thought I'd see a woman who bakes cakes and adorns windows as a role model, but Martha knows how to work the system, and so do I. When I'm out of here, I'll apply for jobs in every loudly liberal English department at every liberal college in America, and I'll use their mission statements to further my case. What better way to publicly demonstrate their commitment to diversity than to welcome a new faculty member who'd lost years of her life to an unjust accusation and a creaky, inept, inherently racist and sexist court system? Yale might be a good place to start; any campus that welcomes a former Taliban member to its student body would have a hard time defending its hypocrisy if it refused to interview an oft-published scholar who'd been falsely accused of a crime five, ten, twenty years earlier.

And what do I do until then? I'm thinking I'll take some grad courses in sociology. I should have no trouble getting into Ann Arbor's program, and the training will be useful for the book I'm planning to write about my fellow convicts. It wouldn't be the first time a scholar has crossed disciplines and gotten exciting new things started...Jacques Derrida made the move from philosophy to literary studies, and though his brand of deconstruction is dated in the extreme, there's no denying the contributions he made to both disciplines.

And while I wait for the appeal process to run its course, I suppose I'll also pass the time talking about nothing with my mindless, goalless, soulless cellmates; reading whatever decent thing I can get my hands on; and writing letters to supposed friends who are too busy to write back and have too little to say when they do.

Six months now, and I still can't shake the surreal feeling that I'm living inside a TV set. Will it ever go away?

A. B.

Dr. John Althorp

[Excerpts from *The Mendham Journal*, Mendham College's weekly newspaper]

** PAID ADVERTISEMENT **

We, the members of the Society for Social Justice, are tired of sitting idly on the sidelines while the faculty and administration of Mendham College withdraw their support of English Department Professor Annette Bain, falsely accused of premeditated murder.

We argue the following:

* Dr. Bain, a world-renowned scholar and the most highly respected member of the English faculty, deserves the support of this institution in her quest to prove her innocence;

* Mendham College Dean John Althorp and President Maurice Harrington have actively withheld information from the student body and faculty regarding the proceedings instituted to revoke Dr. Bain's tenure while she languishes, falsely accused, in prison;

* Members of the Society for Social Justice are experiencing subtle harassment from and discrimination by senior members of the faculty and administration as a result of their support of Dr. Bain.

The administration is hereby warned: We will not allow Mendham College to become a fascist state where innocent people are persecuted on the basis of circumstantial evidence, information is actively and consistently hidden from the Mendham College community, and students are discriminated against on the basis of their beliefs.

[News Story]

Dean Althorp Promoted to Provost
by Kerry Levine
Staff Writer

Dean of Humanities John Althorp, who served in that position for the last five years, has been promoted to Provost of Mendham College. He replaces former provost Marshall Laughton, who has retired after 30 years of service to the college.

In his new job, Dr. Althorp will oversee the curricula of all four of the college's schools of study: humanities, sciences, family studies, and social work.

"Dr. Althorp is the ideal person to direct the programs of study at our fine institution," said President Maurice Harrington. "He combines the greatest of respect for tradition with an open-mindedness about the future of education and students' ever-evolving needs as they negotiate the uncertainties of the twenty-first century. There is no better person to help Mendham College steer a course toward the future while keeping us true to everything we've been in the past."

"We couldn't be happier," said Doctor Gretel Liebtrau, a long-time colleague of Dr. Althorp's in the English department. "We greatly regret that we'll be losing a fine classroom teacher and a wonderful colleague in the department, but our loss is the university's gain. The time has come to share John, and share we must."

Dr. Althorp could not be happier, either. "I feel proud and honored to be named Provost, and I look forward to helping Mendham remain a close-knit academic community while welcoming innovation and change." To that end, Dr. Althorp says, he will work across the schools of study to create new interdisciplinary majors in global political/economic studies, social justice studies, and women's studies.

Dr. Althorp received his B.A. from Mendham College in 1973, then returned to teach here after receiving his Ph.D. at New York University in 1978. He is married and has two daughters.

[Lead story]

Annette Bain Found Dead in Prison
by Josh Finkel
Staff Writer

The faculty, staff, and student body of Mendham College were shocked to learn on Monday that disgraced English professor Annette Bain had been found dead in her prison cell, an apparent suicide. While all of the details are not yet clear, it is known that a security guard named Merydith Clarkson found Dr. Bain hanging in her cell. It appeared that Dr. Bain had pushed her cot against the cell bars, then used a noose created from bed sheets and a blanket to hang herself. She was pronounced dead on arrival at the prison hospital by Dr. Roberto Carrione.

According to the *New York Times*, however, there are several mysterious facts that do not add up. There had been no indication that Dr. Bain was at all depressed or despondent. As reported in these pages, she'd been extremely active in her defense; drove the appeals process with the assistance of her attorney, Marcia McClellan; and had recently been accepted into a highly regarded graduate sociology program. Reports from inside the prison indicate that Dr. Bain had a very unpleasant relationship with Merydith Clarkson, as well as frequent run-ins with a fellow inmate named Kim Baxter, who has a history of violence and who has been accused twice of killing other inmates. An investigation into all these matters is pending.

Dr. Bain was serving a twenty-five-year sentence for the murder of Detective Joseph Castro, whom she stabbed to death in his Queens home last year. Despite overwhelming evidence of her guilt, she always maintained her innocence.

A memorial service for Dr. Bain will be held in Grady Auditorium on Friday evening at 7:30 p.m.

Nick Lang

Just as he'd done when they were partners, Nick followed Joe's instructions. First he went to the mail stop and retrieved two letters from box 175, one from Annette Bain and one from Betty Lewis. Then he read through the contents of each filing cabinet drawer in alphabetical order.

As always, Joe had been extremely methodical in the way he'd chosen to organize and file the information he'd collected. Each of the five drawers held color-coded file folders with the same neatly handwritten labels. In a red file marked CORRE-SPONDENCE he found copies of the letters "A" had sent to B, C, D, and E, as well as the individual letters written by each assassin. As Joe would have done, Nick filed the recently retrieved letters from B and D in their respective folders.

A blue file labeled ASSASSIN held information that Joe had amassed about B, C, D, and E—their identities, addresses, habits, hangouts, and quirks, all reported with the same meticulous orientation to detail that characterized Joe's detective reports. Each ASSASSIN folder also held dozens of photos. Nick assumed that Joe had snapped many of the pictures as he'd staked out the individual P.O. boxes in place like MailStopUSA and Mail24, waiting for each assassin to pick up his or her letters of instruction. Other snapshots showed the assassins in other locales: at their places of employment, going into and coming out of their apartments and houses, and in various stores and other public facilities.

The yellow files, labeled VICTIM, held information about each assassin's target or "chosen," including photographs. Based on the details provided in the assassins' letters of instruction/ explanation/rationalization, it had been quite easy for Joe to find the intended victims, observe them from close or medium range, and snap photos when they weren't looking. Joe had also written a detailed report on each one, outlining the chosen's comings, goings, and daily rituals.

Nick noted with something close to approval that Joe hadn't excluded himself from the appropriate ASSASSIN and VICTIM file folders. Nick remained stone-faced as he flipped through photos of Joe in various poses—lifting weights in the gym; in uniform during his early days as a beat cop; standing on the sidelines in his coach's gear at a soccer game, screaming at some unseen referee or player who hadn't performed according to expectations. Each photo presented a facet of the man, Nick thought, but it was that last picture, the one exhibiting Joe's disproportionate anger and frustration over something as meaningless as a girls' soccer game, that best captured the man's essence.

The green PRESS file folders held newspaper articles about each of the murders, with each individual clipping carefully taped to a sheet of 8.5" x 11" paper. Printouts from various Internet news sources were also included. The killing of Jesse Garanowicz/Teddy Boyle had received far and away the most press attention; the folder held everything from news articles to opinion pieces to letters to the editor.

To determine if Joe had stored any information electronically, Nick had tried turning on Joe's computer and accessing his files, but the start-up routine was aborted each time he incorrectly guessed Joe's password. *Might as well throw the computer out*, Nick thought, though he suspected that the right techie might be able to unlock its secrets.

So much for the much-vaunted double-blind system Joe had offered his partners in crime. His letters had vowed complete confidentiality in strong and confident terms, promising that even the mastermind known as "A" wouldn't know what was happening or to whom. But Joe had kept copies of everything, proving...what exactly? That his original plan (which had obviously taken an extremely unexpected turn) had been to see the murders carried out, to "solve" that slew of seemingly unrelated crimes, and then to write his book, thus gaining glory and renown for himself?

And did the assassins' naïveté prove that criminals, and people in general, are as ignorant and stupid as Joe had always believed them to be? You'd have to be beyond simple to think you could trust a man you'd never met to keep your murderous secret. But Joe had always been a charmer, a manipulator, and his letters to B, C, D, and E had been most authoritative and persuasive. Joe knew how to work desperate, guilty people—Nick had seen him break lying witnesses in record time. In fact, watching Joe Castro grill a suspect was a pastime at the precinct house. Many a rookie had learned more from watching Joe through the two-way glass than he could have learned in a lifetime of classroom training. Joe sensed what made people tick, he understood their vulnerabilities, and he had an almost psychic sense of how to exploit those weaknesses. He was the ultimate con man, convincing murderers and rapists he was their friend before smashing their heads into the concrete floor. If Joe could con criminals so well, why should Nick—or anyone else, for that matter—be surprised that he was equally skilled at conning civilians desperate to rid themselves of an unpleasant aspect of their lives?

As he always did during the course of an investigation, Nick summarized his key findings on a single sheet of paper.

C: Leo Lentricchia, Throgs Neck NY
    Works for phone company
    Killed: Freddy d'Arget, Bloomfield NJ − drug dealer,
       murdered in house with blunt object to head

Plotted against future brother-in-law Roger Borelli,
Throgs Neck, NY – shot in the head by Joe

D: Annette Bain, Manhattan
English professor at Mendham College
Killed: Joe – poisoned him, then stabbed him 78 times
Plotted against John Althorp, president of Mendham
College – murder never carried out

E: Father Tomás Rodriguez, Queens
Parish priest at St. Elizabeth Parish, Astoria
Killed: no one
Plotted against Joe

Drawer A had prepared Nick for what he would learn as he read through the contents of the next four drawers. It included a copy of the original newspaper ad from *The Clarion*, as well as Joe's book proposal and correspondence with his agent, who, it seemed, had sold the book to Joan Ventre, a senior editor at Manor House. The last file folder in that drawer was labeled "FOR NICK," and it included a letter in a sealed envelope.

As Nick read through Drawer A, he thought that Joe's double life wasn't as much of a surprise to him as it would have been to some of the other guys on the squad, or even to Sharon or Eileen. Nick had heard the rumors about Joe and the Manhattan hookers, Joe and the local bar owners, and Joe and the girls who worked at various strip clubs. He'd seen Joe "accidentally" shoot a fleeing suspect through the heart instead of the leg, then lie about it on the witness stand. And Nick too had lied on the witness stand, backing up Joe's story because that was what partners did for each other.

And he understood Joe's frustration with criminals, and society's inability to deal with them, because it was a frustration that Nick, and all other detectives, shared. No matter how much you did, no matter how hard you tried, at the end of the day almost everyone got away with everything, either because they got lucky or because one of a million loopholes set them free. Even those who went to prison hardly suffered for their crimes, what with the hours spent in the weight room, the three square meals a day, and the host of other programs designed to keep criminals happy enough to prevent them from killing the guards. Was it any wonder Joe had decided to take matters into his own hands? He'd wanted to get Jesse Garanowicz taken care of, and the method he'd chosen had proven extremely effective, at zero cost to taxpayers.

A: Joe Castro, Queens
     NYC Detective
     Killed: Roger Borelli
     Plotted against Jesse Garanowicz/Teddy Boyle, convict-
         ed pedophile living in Brooklyn
     Killed by Annette Bain

The contents of Drawer B had surprised Nick much more than the contents of Drawer A. At first, looking through the photos in the ASSASSIN file, he'd thought Joe had concocted an elaborate joke, like the Tristero in *The Crying of Lot 49*. For there she was, his aunt Betty—really a cousin, not an aunt—in all her mundane glory: incognito in sunglasses and a hat as she retrieved her letters of instruction from her P.O. boxes; sporting gardening gloves as she pruned the rose bushes in her back-yard; wearing her typical frumpy clothing as she placed a jar of store-brand wheat germ into her shopping basket.

But it all made sense by the time he'd finished reading the contents of Drawer E. She'd told Nick about—and asked for his help with—her drug-dealing neighbor, and Freddy d'Arget was

now dead, thanks to the *Clarion* ad, Joe Castro, and Leo
Lentricchia. As Nick read his aunt's gleeful narrative detailing
her execution of Jesse Garanowicz with poisoned Girl Scout
cookies, he found himself impressed with the old girl's nerve.
His entire life, he'd thought of her as ineffectual Aunt Betty,
the old maid who'd taken care of her beastly mother until she'd
died and who was barely scraping by in a tiny house in Jersey.
But as he read her letter, she was transformed into something
quite different: neighborhood watchdog, avenging angel, and
remorseless double murderess.

If Joe had known B was related to his partner, he'd given no
indication of that in the drawer devoted to Betty Lewis's life
and crimes. Nick wasn't sure he'd ever mentioned having an
aunt in Jersey to Joe. Perhaps if Nick had gone to visit Aunt
Betty more, or talked about her once in a while, Joe would have
made the connection.

B: Betty Lewis, Bloomfield, NJ
    Secretary at insurance firm in NYC
    Killed: Jesse Garanowicz/Teddy Boyle
    Plotted against Freddy d'Arget, drug dealer/neighbor
        (killed by Leo Lentricchia)

And now, with so many of the questions about Joe's death
answered, Nick realized that one important question remained:
What should he do with the information gleaned from the filing
cabinet?

He could do what Joe had planned to do: pretend to be the
brilliant investigative mind who discovered the links among
these supposedly unrelated murders, then use his notoriety for
promotions, fame, and fortune. Certainly, sharing some of the
information from the filing cabinet with the right people
would further his career, get him that promotion and raise he

wanted and deserved—the same promotion for which Aunt Betty had been encouraging him to fight. Finally he'd get to be in charge instead of being Joe's, or some other senior detective's, lackey. But such a promotion would likely come at the price of a lifetime prison sentence for an old woman who was mostly harmless.

He could write a book of his own, maybe sell it to Hollywood for a million dollars. But he didn't know how to write, and besides—*The Everyday Killer* was Joe's book, not his. To expose the truth would be to expose not only Joe's crimes but also Joe's private life, and he couldn't do that—he couldn't let Joe's neighbors, the parents of the kids he coached, and the people of St. Elizabeth's know who Joe really was and why he allowed himself to be murdered. Telling only part of the story wouldn't work, either, as the inevitable questions would ultimately lead someone, somewhere to discover the complete truth. The subsequent media circus would be a nightmare for everyone involved in law enforcement in New York City, and perhaps the nation, as the unquestioned and unquestioning solidarity of the men in blue came under fire.

Justice is much simpler than anyone allows it to be, Joe had written in the last paragraph of his letter to Nick. *So make it happen, however you see fit.*

And there was Joe again, controlling the situation from beyond the grave.

* * *

Nick turned his unmarked Buick off the Major Deegan Expressway onto the East 233rd Street exit in the Bronx. Within five minutes, he had spied the work crew, a group of five men closely inspecting a metallic green box located near the rear entrance to a small industrial park. A large Transamerica Communications van was parked nearby.

He recognized Leo immediately from the photographs in Joe's filing cabinet. The thick head with crew cut, the drooping mouth, the saggy eyes...Leo looked much dumber in person than he did in the photos, in which he'd come across as more malevolent and, perhaps, more intelligent. A man who appeared to be in charge called a break, and the five guys grabbed their coolers and lunch sacks from the back of the van, then made their way to a small picnic table at the edge of the property. As the guys talked, Nick observed. Leo sat at the edge of the table, occasionally putting in a word or two but mostly nodding at the other men's conversation and laughing at their jokes. Occasionally he made conversation with the guy sitting across from him, a redhead who looked twice Leo's age.

Nick got out of the car and strode purposefully to the picnic table.

"Hey, guys."

The workers stopped talking, taken aback by the civilian who'd interrupted their meal.

"How you doing today?" Nick asked.

"Good, man," said the foreman. "Something we can do for ya?"

"Actually, there is. Hey, Leo."

Leo glared at the stranger. "Yeah, what is it?"

"I'm wondering if you're ever gonna tell your buddies here about the way you hired someone to kill Roger Borelli."

"W-what? What the fuck are you talking about?" Leo stammered.

"You know what I'm talking about, Leo. Now tell Roger's friends here how you hired someone to kill him. I'll leave so you can do it in private."

Thirty seconds later, Nick was driving through the streets of the North Central Bronx looking for a mailbox. He finally found one and dropped in the letter he'd written the night before. The letter was addressed to "Giovanni S. Lentricchia, 4271 ■■■■■■■■■ Avenue, Throgs Neck, NY, 10465."

Dear Mr. Lentricchia –

Your son Leo arranged for the murder of Roger Borelli. I know this for a fact. Do something about it, or I will. You have one week.

A Friend

* * *

Annette Bain had been taken care of, with the help of Merydith and Big Kim, even before Nick discovered the filing cabinet in Joe Castro's attic.

That left just one person to visit.

Martha Goldstein

Sipping her vodka martini, Martha Goldstein looked at her friends and thought how grateful she was that none of them really cared about her.

They were sitting on the veranda of the restaurant at the Boca Raton Golf Club, nibbling on a light lunch and chatting about nothing while their husbands exerted intense amounts of money, energy, and time into steering small white balls into cups a few hundred yards away. *Does anyone actually* enjoy *this game?* Martha wondered. Sol usually came home from the club angry and frustrated, even when he'd played a good game and the weather had been divine. The men he played with weren't his friends any more than these women were her friends. They were simply people of similar ages, backgrounds, and incomes, living in the same community and looking for other people to gossip about and impress.

She vaguely remembered the days when she'd had friends of a more traditional variety. She'd always been a pretty girl, a quality much valued by the old Philadelphia Main Line families and one that had guaranteed her as many party invitations as she could accept. She'd had some close girlfriends in her school days (though she couldn't remember their names just now), girls with summer homes and eligible brothers. But from an early age they all shared the tacit understanding that their friendships were temporary. Your coming out as a debutante was the biggest step you'd take away from your girlfriends, and once you crossed that threshold, there was no turning back. Such a break was inevitable given the intense competition for the best boys, with your mother and your former friends' mothers carefully managing your path toward marriage, family, and tradition.

It had been an elegant world, full of drafty old homes and expensive but shabby Oriental carpets and libraries filled with aging books, bourbon, and gin. A far cry from the tacky, over-priced, hideously ugly mini-mansions of Boca Raton Estates, the gated community in which they all lived and bedded one another as if they were randy teenagers discovering sex rather than sun-dried, wrinkled fifty- and sixty-somethings with moles, flab, and hair in the wrong places. Martha didn't belong in this world of hideously botoxed and face-lifted gargoyles and their controlling, Viagra-addicted men; she belonged in a world of refinement and culture. But the Northeast was so cold, and the area so horribly congested, and the people so increasingly tacky, even at the best clubs and in the best neighborhoods. The global economy had allowed an influx of the wealthy from every obscure kingdom and emirate into just about every exclusive neighborhood that had once existed in the Northeast, and while *those people* might have had the money to buy their way in, they certainly didn't share the same values on which Martha had been raised.

So, in the aftermath of *the trouble*, why not escape to a warmer, simpler climate? Her husband, a horribly weak man, hadn't been able to cope with the media, the phone calls, the blow to the family's reputation. Dying had been the easy way out, the simple choice. There hadn't been as much money as she'd thought, and her financial advisor had told her she wouldn't be able to stay in the house, which she didn't want to do anyway. She was damaged goods in the Northeast. No widower, knowing what everyone knew about her monstrous offspring, would even think about taking her out, much less marrying her. She had to go where she wouldn't be known—where eligible, financially secure men of her age would be taken by her still-pretty face and still-perky bosom. For weeks before her move, she'd shaken and shivered when thinking about what she'd have to do when she arrived in the Sunshine State. But she was a strong woman, a survivor. She had to take care of herself. No one else was going to.

And so Martha Garanowicz sold her house, changed her legal name to Martha Gray, and moved herself into a well-appointed cottage in Boca Raton. She put herself in circulation—her mother had trained her well in that regard more than forty years earlier—and started keeping company with Sol Goldstein, a twice-divorced importer of cheap clothing made in Far Eastern sweatshops. Like all the men in Boca, he was loud and crass, a self-styled alpha male who basked in the power of his money but was self-conscious about his skinny legs and growing bald spot. Spending time with Sol was torture, but she said the required "I love you's" and made love to him vigorously. Really, sex wasn't *that* much of a price to pay for having a roof over her head, a new BMW every couple of years, and plenty of spending money, but she was getting to the age where lovemaking just seemed like too much bother. Still, she expected that her fate was to continue pretending to enjoy sex with Sol three times a week until he dropped dead of a heart attack.

As far as Sol knew, she was just another youngish slightly impoverished widow from Pennsylvania. She'd perfected her story before taking residence in Boca: Her husband had died of a heart attack, and her only son had died of meningitis as a teenager. Such story telling came to her naturally, the ability to lie quickly and easily about unpleasant parts of one's past being an essential skill required of those from good families. She'd briefly thought about saying she'd never had any children, but Jesse had been born via C-section and those scars couldn't be explained any other way. She had some old albums full of photographs in case Sol ever got curious, but he never did. She belonged to him now. Her past didn't matter, and the present was full of responsibilities to his four children from his two previous marriages and his seven grandchildren, all of whom seemed to descend on Boca the second Daylight Savings Time ended.

She knew that many of her friends from Boca Raton Estates lived the same generic lives, spending their husbands' money by day, serving their sexual needs at night, and catering to their children and grandchildren on vacations and holidays. More specific information was usually gleaned via gossip sessions when one of the friends was absent. She heard about Aimee's husband's indiscretions with the housekeeper courtesy of Norma and Louise. In turn, Aimee had gossiped with Martha about Louise's addiction to a certain little pill, and both Louise and Aimee had not been reluctant to share the details regarding Norma's disturbing tendency to stalk a well-regarded physician at whom she'd thrown herself on more than one occasion, and whose caller ID box provided ample evidence of Norma's unwanted attentions.

Martha knew what her friends said about her behind her back: she drank too much, she was verbally abusive to sales clerks, she'd performed oral sex on a policeman who'd visited her home as part of a routine investigation after a house in the Estates had been robbed. All these things were true. She felt the need to create intrigue around herself, to occasionally let juicy tidbits slip to her closest friends so that the gossip mill would remain active. With a steady stream of quasi-salacious information coming their way, nobody would think to dig any deeper.

All these quirks and indiscretions were smokescreens to keep people from discovering Jesse. And she intended to keep Jesse a secret until her dying day.

She hadn't thought about him much in recent years. Jesse was a grown man, and she'd given him significant financial backing, which was more than many of her friends could say they'd done for *their* children. Besides, she didn't come from a place where parents and their adult children were on top of one another every minute of every day—unlike her Boca Estates neighbors, those transplanted Jews and Italians from New York and New Jersey who talked to their adult children ten times a day via cell phone. You raised your children to become adults, and then they became responsible for their own lives. Your obligations ended after you sent them to college and set them up. Period.

Still, a certain amount of upset is to be expected when one turns on the evening news and hears that one's only child, a convicted child molester living in Brooklyn, has been found dead in his apartment. The newscaster's distaste mirrored Martha's own as he reported the circumstances surrounding the discovery of the body: The residents of Jesse's condo building could no longer ignore the smell of his rotting carcass and had called the police, who'd found Jesse's body lying in the middle of his kitchen floor. From subsequent news reports and a trip to the library, where she could use the computer without worrying that Sol would walk in as she surfed the Net, she garnered additional details about the poisoned Girl Scout cookies, which had apparently been loaded with a poison so toxic that Jesse had probably died within 15 seconds of eating his first Samoa. That was some consolation—at least he hadn't suffered.

In most ways, the death was a blessing. Jesse's life couldn't have been happy, and perhaps he was now in a better place. Even better, she would no longer have to fear that her son would somehow find her, call her, or show up on her doorstep. But her relief was almost instantly replaced with anxiety. The authorities would certainly be searching for his next of kin, and it wouldn't be difficult to find her. The last thing she needed was a police officer showing up at the house with Sol home, somberly announcing her son's death in front of her husband.

She decided to be proactive. She made phone calls to the right people and identified herself. She asked Sol if she could go to New York for a few days to see some theatre, do some shopping, and visit her old friend Vera. She'd lost touch with the real Vera decades earlier, but she occasionally manufactured stories about her fellow Bryn Mawr alum just to have an excuse to get out of Boca if she ever needed to. Sol granted his permission, and off she flew to New York to sign papers and attend to the details. They'd asked her if she'd wanted to see the body while advising her that it was a disturbing sight. She'd declined on the grounds that she just couldn't handle it.

She'd been worried about what she might find in Jesse's apartment, but the police had already taken anything that might prove what sorts of activities he'd been up to. She sold the condo and its contents at an unbelievably low price to a greedy realtor who paid cash, then deposited the monies in a secret account in which she'd long been hoarding money. Then she went to lower Fifth Avenue, bought some expensive handbags and shoes, and went out for a lovely meal at which she drank too much. She spent the evening in her room at the W Union Square hotel vomiting, then flew back to Boca the following morning.

The trip to New York had taken place two weeks ago, and life was now back to normal: lunches at the club, dinner parties, her husband's children and grandchildren. She'd been a little shaky since her return, but because none of these people—not her husband, not her friends, not her neighbors—paid one ounce of attention to anyone but themselves, no one had noticed that she'd been on edge or drinking more than usual.

What would they say if they knew about Jesse? Nothing directly, of course. But her friends would begin pulling away and her husband would find a pretext to divorce her, as a tarnished trophy wife is easily replaced with someone newer and shinier. And she was too old start over somewhere else.

Listening to Norma, Aimee, and Louise prattle on about wines they knew nothing about, she felt a combination of rage and indignity. Why did she care what these idiots thought? They were nothing more than cheap whores with big hair and too much jewelry who'd spread their legs and married well. In fact, it was the behavior of women—people—like them who'd gotten Jesse into trouble. She pictured Louise as a ten-year-old flirt, cockteasing the mailman; Aimee as an eight-year old girl grinding herself into her favorite uncle's knee; Norma as a young girl wearing short shorts and brushing up against her favorite teacher. Children *are* sexual, Martha knew, and they could be the seducers as well as the seducees. She herself had been sexually active at a young age with the father of one of her friends; the technical term might be statutory rape, but she knew that what he'd done to her hadn't been completely against her will. She wondered if any of the children who'd accused Jesse had started the sort of thing with her son that she herself had started with her friend's father. She wouldn't have been surprised if they had.

Tomás Rodriguez

After more than a year of worrying about Tomás's declining health, Father Declan Moriarty, pastor of the Church of St. Elizabeth, had decided to act. He'd called his superior to recommend that Tomás be given a furlough from conducting mass and performing the community services to which he'd devoted himself since coming to the parish three years earlier.

The first year Declan had watched with marvel and awe as Tomás, the oldest son of a wealthy and devout Puerto Rican sugar cane farmer, threw himself into his duties. Tomás became a trusted friend of the parishioners immediately, a man whose appearance at the elementary school made the children squeal with delight. His homilies, always considered and thoughtful, had focused on not only the Catholic's personal relationship with Jesus but also with other humans, as mothers, fathers, brothers, sisters, friends, and teachers. Best of all, Tomás's charisma made it easy for him to conscript volunteers to help with church carnivals and charity work, which made Declan Moriarty's life infinitely easier. On occasion Declan experienced thunderbolts of insecurity as he saw Tomás's popularity eclipse his own, but he still prayed nightly that the diocese would allow Tomás to remain at St. Elizabeth's permanently—or at least until Declan retired to that wonderful estate in upstate New York, far from the crowds, the grime, and the considerable financial and emotional needs of St. Elizabeth's parishioners.

But Tomás had clearly taken on too much. He involved himself in so many activities, and kept himself so busy, that he neglected to nourish himself. His homilies had become increasingly abstract and rambling, sometimes even mystical, and often filled with denunciations of the sins of pride, gluttony, sloth, and arrogance. Such sermons had gone out of fashion decades earlier, and people in the community of St. Elizabeth had begun to whisper that Father Tomás was working too hard and perhaps needed a rest.

I mustn't be selfish, Declan had scolded himself. *Tomás has given himself to me and this parish. It is time for us to give back to him. No matter that I will have to work harder, much harder, than I do now. When Tomás has been nursed back to health, he will be able to resume his calling with renewed vigor.*

Declan had finally placed the call after Tomás fainted on the grammar school's staircase. He'd collapsed and tumbled down the stairs, injuring his skull and bruising the rest of his body quite badly. After a stint in the hospital, Tomás had begged to be allowed to return to the rectory, where he hoped he could read and pray in solitude, with his closest friends within earshot if he needed them.

Clarence Benson, Declan's superior, had been instrumental in bringing Tomás to New York City from his native Puerto Rico and was quite fond of both the young priest and Declan, with whom he had studied in seminary. He listened with concern as Declan provided a detailed account of Tomás's increasingly manic behavior and what appeared to be a physical condition similar to anorexia.

"In confidence, Declan," Father Benson began tentatively, "this is the third time this has happened. Tomás had his first breakdown after two years in a difficult San Juan parish. He needed time away from the city, so after his recovery we sent him to a much quieter parish in Ponce. But after two years there, he had another breakdown. Eventually he asked to come to the States, and the powers that be said yes. Everyone agreed that it was a good idea to get him away from the place his father had been murdered."

Declan's mouth dropped open in shock. Tomás's father had been murdered? Tomás had never spoken of that horrible occurrence—never.

Declan decided to focus on his concern for Tomás rather than his anger at Clarence for not sharing this information with him earlier.

"My God, Clarence, what happened?"

"Mr. Rodriguez was a rich man whose wealth and power were widely envied. One of the men on his plantation, a man he'd recently hired, was very resentful of his low wages. One day he had too much to drink on the job, and he sprang on Tomás's father with a machete. Dozens of people saw him hacking the man to death, screaming 'power to the people' and 'the poor will rise up.' The next day, the man was found dead in a ditch, shot execution style. He'd been castrated before being shot."

Declan was momentarily speechless. When he recovered, he made his request. "Clarence, let Tomás rest for a few months at the rectory. Please. This is where he wants to be, and I want to keep an eye on him. When he's better, we need someone more skilled than I am to talk to him about...these other things."

* * *

Now Declan found himself knocking lightly on the door of his friend's private quarters. The visitor had been insistent. When Tomás heard his name, he asked Declan to bring the visitor upstairs for a brief visit.

"Come in," Tomás said quietly. He was sitting in a faded easy chair reading the Bible, wearing a pair of old blue jeans and a flannel shirt, both of which were too large for his emaciated frame.

Declan opened the door. "Tomás, this is Detective Lang."

"It's good to meet you, Detective Lang. I wish we could have met under better circumstances."

"Call me Nick."

"I'll leave you two to talk," Declan said, backing out of the room. He'd made it abundantly clear to Detective Lang that he was not to say or do anything that would upset Tomás—and that his visit was to last no longer than ten minutes.

Nick sat in a small hard chair facing Tomás Rodriguez, the priest who'd arranged for the murder of his partner through a dead bitch of an English professor.

"Words fail me, Nick," Tomás said quietly. "Joe's death was a terrible loss for all of us. I'm sure you've heard that many times."

Nick's field of vision went dark for a second. He held his breath, fighting his desire to leap from his chair, wrap his hands around the frail young priest's throat, and squeeze until Tomás Rodriguez was as dead as Joe Castro and Annette Bain.

"Father, you don't need to talk. I just want you to listen. OK?" Tomás nodded.

"I'm not good with words, Father, but I feel like I owe this to Joe. That's why I'm here. He would have wanted me to talk to you. I'm doing this for him."

Nick took a breath and continued with the lie. "Joe and I were close, you know? He told me everything, or almost everything. We were like brothers. But you know what, Father? I could never compete with you."

"I don't understand...."

"I don't have brothers and sisters, Father. I'm an only child. Joe was like the brother I never had. I wanted him to look up to me. I couldn't stand it that the person he looked up to the most was you, not me."

"I...I don't know what to say...."

"You don't have to say anything, Father. Joe would never have told you this himself. He idolized you. I can't tell you how many times he told me he wished he could be more like you. He envied you, Father. He knew what his problems were, and he wished he could be kind and giving like you. I know you've been sick, and I thought it would make you feel better to hear this. That's why I'm here. You deserve to know. You've done a lot of good, Father, more than you can imagine. You touched the life of a man for the better. I thought that knowing how Joe felt would help you, the way you helped him."

Tomás Rodriguez was silent for a moment. "Thank you, Nick. Thank you for telling me."

"I had to do it, Father. But while I'm here, I wonder if I could ask you for a favor."

"Yes. Anything."

"I've been in touch with a cousin of Joe's. He's really broken up about Joe and he needs to talk to someone. Would you talk to him, Father? If you helped Joe, you can help him. I'm not good with this stuff. I don't know what to say to him. But you will. Can I have him call you?"

"Yes, Nick. Of course." Tomás grabbed a pad and pencil from the small table next to the reading chair, scribbled something on the top sheet, and tore it off. "Here's my phone number. Please, tell him to call me any time. I can talk with him on the phone, or he can come here to meet me. Or I'll ask someone to drive me to wherever he lives."

"Thank you, Father. I should let you rest now."

"Thank you, Nick. Thank you for coming."

Nick stood and turned to leave. Tomás extended his hand and Nick shook it, crushing it so hard he felt bones break. But Tomás didn't wince.

"Oh, Father. I forgot to tell you. Joe's cousin's name is John Althorp. Dr. John Althorp. This way, you'll know who he is when he calls."

* * *

The next morning, Declan stopped at Tomás's private quarters rather earlier than usual. The woman who cooked for them had just told him that Tomás hadn't eaten anything from the tray she'd brought him the previous evening. This alarmed Declan, as it was clearly a step in the wrong direction. Tomás's appetite had improved ever so slightly in the previous week, and he didn't want Tomás to begin a downhill slide.

When Tomás didn't respond to his knock, Declan became alarmed. He tried turning the doorknob, which was locked.

Sensing something very wrong, Declan ran to the rectory office, retrieved the key from the safe, ran back to Tomás's room, and unlocked the door, his hands shaking. Tomás was slumped in his chair, his closed Bible in his lap. An empty pill bottle sat on the reading table next to him.

Also on the table were two sheets of paper that had been pulled from the notepad.

NICK: I AM SORRY.

DECLAN: FORGIVE ME. YOU WILL NOT SEE ME IN HEAVEN.

Nick Lang

One remaining dilemma faced Detective Nicholas Lang. In his mind he'd been using the same terminology Joe had coined, so it made sense to frame the final question in the words Joe would have used. How should he complete the circle?

He considered the likely outcome of the circle of assassins if Joe hadn't been the victim of his own plot. The man on whom Aunt Betty had taken out a very unconventional contract was a lowlife of epic proportions, the kind of man who should have died of a drug overdose or in a drive-by shooting years earlier. But like a cat Freddy d'Arget had nine lives, and he'd used every one of those lives to make the world a more terrible place. Earth, North America, the United States, the East Coast, New Jersey, the town of Bloomfield—none of them were worse off because Freddy d'Arget's brains had been bashed in by a lumbering moron from Throgs Neck, New York. Maybe the druggies and scumbags whom Freddy had supplied had been slightly inconvenienced, having to find a new dealer on short notice. But that wouldn't have taken very long, as plenty of aspiring drug lords always seemed to be waiting in the wings. And it wasn't as if Freddy had a devoted family mourning the death of their precious boy. He'd been alone in the world—no caring friends, no loving children, not even a concerned co-worker.

He couldn't fault his aunt for the tough choice she'd made. He'd read all the materials Joe had collected about Freddy, and after he'd paid his visit to Father Tomás, he'd continued his research. Every news article and court report confirmed Joe's opinion of Freddy as a lowlife enabled by a liberal system to continue doing and dealing drugs. Everyone knows the police don't actively seek out the murderers of drug dealers, and nobody of consequence argues with such inaction. Society has scarce resources; choices have to be made, and money must be spent where it will do the most good. People whose lives had value and meaning deserve to have their murderers sought and brought to justice. People whose lives were devoted to the diminishment of mankind deserve to rot where their dead bodies lie.

His aunt had taken the only action she had the power to take. The police, the courts, the legal system—and he, Nick Lang himself—had failed her and the people of ■■■■ ■■■■■■■ Road. Betty Lewis had no choice but to take the law into her own hands.

He couldn't work up any indignation regarding her murder of Jesse Garanowicz, either. That was another case where she'd done the world a favor, ridding it of a man who would surely have raped and killed more children before someone finally managed to put him away. Joe had been obsessed with the Garanowicz case, and for good reason: It embodied the frustrations that all members of law enforcement feel every day of their working lives. New York City's cops and detectives came mostly from working class backgrounds. They were the Irish, the Italians, the Jews whose parents had scrimped and saved so their kids could attend affordable schools like CUNY and Queens College. They knew what it was like to work for a living—they had no choice in the matter. So they worked long hours of overtime, and when they retired with a full pension funded by the taxpayers, they knew they'd earned every penny. They supported their families and respected their neighbors, just as their parents had taught them to. But every day they encountered people who fancied themselves the upper class—snotty idiots with degrees from Columbia and Yale, schools that exist to perpetuate an elite and elitist class. These were the big-hearted liberals, living in their Central Park penthouses thanks to their huge trust funds. They were the do-gooders who thought rapists should be forgiven because their father hadn't loved them enough, and that vicious murderers should be released because a beat cop somewhere hadn't followed a minor procedure with the proper degree of precision. And if you were a criminal lucky enough to have money, you could afford one their friends from those same overpriced schools, money-grubbing lawyers whose sole goal was to enrich themselves by getting criminals off the hook.

Was it any wonder that working, honest, desperate, powerless people sometimes said "enough is enough"? All their lives they'd been told what to do, where to go, how to behave. They'd punched clocks and paid their taxes. They'd been given parking and speeding tickets to help the city make up for the budget shortfalls created by crooked politicians. They were put on hold every time they called their utility or credit card company. They waited in line at the DMV for hours, only to be dismissed at the window for not having the correct form filled out. They lost their jobs so the same millionaire, billionaire, trillionaire Harvard graduates could make another million by shipping their operations overseas.

And yet they didn't complain, at least not loudly enough, or not enough en masse, to see any improvements. They could be content as long as they had their small house, or comfortable apartment, to go home to. But even then they could never be sure some government agency wouldn't come along and put a halfway house in the middle of their block or a housing project in their backyard. And if the government chose to house criminals and sex offenders among them, there was nothing they could do about it. Nothing. They didn't have the money to hire lawyers, and they didn't have the money to move somewhere else. But they didn't want to move. They wanted to stay in their homes, where they had lived in peace until the drug dealer, the wife beater, or the gang members moved in.

His Aunt Betty had done the right thing her entire life. She'd taken care of that miserly, difficult mother of hers until the day she died. If she'd known about her mother's money, she could have moved out of that dump in the Bronx decades earlier than she did. And certainly she would have been able to help him when he'd needed help so desperately. His parents, blue collar like himself, had died when he was seventeen, leaving him nothing but the ratty old furniture in their apartment. He wanted to live with Aunt Betty, at least for a couple of years until he was on his feet, but her bitch mother wouldn't allow it. So there he was, on his own at age seventeen, renting a room from a neighbor, working full time, and attending the John Jay College of Criminal Justice part time. He'd desperately needed help with the tuition, with money for textbooks, but Aunt Betty hadn't had a penny to spare. He remembered how she'd cried when she said she couldn't give him the money—because she simply didn't have it. Her mother's medications were so expensive, she said, and the rent went up every year, and she even went to bed hungry half the time because the food budget was so tight.

But then the mother had died and Aunt Betty had discovered the stash of stocks and bonds, and almost overnight she'd bought the house in Bloomfield. And so, after all those years of struggling, she'd finally gotten herself a tiny house in a good town, only to see the peace of her last years threatened. She was a smart woman, his Aunt Betty—she knew what every suburban homeowner in America knows: When people like Freddy d'Arget move onto your block, it's the beginning of the end.

He wished he'd helped with the Freddy situation when she'd told him about it, months earlier. But he'd been wrapped up in his own life, as he often was, dealing with the drama of yet another series of girlfriends who wanted his time, his commitment, his attention, his blood. He didn't have time for *another* needy woman who wanted him to solve all her problems, implying not so subtly that he somehow owed her his time and services. He'd felt sorry for her, he really had; but he'd had to take care of himself when life threw him a series of unpleasant curve balls, and so did she. Maybe if she'd been willing to fight more with her mother so he could have had a place to live while he went to college, or if she'd ever sent him even a penny, he would have been more willing to take a tip to Bloomfield to talk to the guy—he and Joe could be *very* persuasive when they needed to be. But she'd never helped him, which meant she had no right to demand his help.

And as it turned out, she hadn't needed his help anyway. She'd answered Joe's ad and gotten her problem taken care of. She'd also held up her end of the bargain, dispatching Jesse quickly and cleanly. Nick knew—though the media did not—that the security camera in the lobby of Jesse's building had captured a few grainy images of a woman and a Girl Scout entering the building, as well as other images of the same woman returning with a bag full of cookies a couple of weeks later. But she'd been cagey enough to make sure her back, and the back of her Girl Scout accomplice, were to the camera at all times. He'd seen the freeze frames and recognized his aunt's posture and build, but the police would never be able to identify her from those images. Never.

And he wasn't going to help them. His mind was made up.

He owed this to her. He'd let her down, but perhaps by letting her down he'd done her a favor. He'd given her the incentive she needed to fight the system. After a lifetime of being trampled on, of feeling defenseless and powerless, she'd taken action. And her action had only positive results. So what if two murders had been involved? There were murders that mattered and murders that didn't. Every cop knew this, and so did Aunt Betty: All human life is not equal.

No, let Aunt Betty live out the rest of her life in the house she'd worked so hard for. She deserved it, and besides—she hadn't done anything Nick himself wouldn't have done in the same situation. That letter from Joe, advising him to "make justice happen," had given him the most powerful sense of control he'd ever experienced. That experience was the only gift Joe had ever given him. He suspected that Aunt Betty had probably felt that same sense of control when she ordered the hit on Freddy and concocted her cookie-poisoning scheme to rid the world of a pedophile. Basking in the glow of his power, Nick wasn't about to strip that same feeling away from a woman who'd lived much longer, and suffered much more, than he had.

So what if parts of her story didn't quite add up? In her initial letter to Joe, she'd mentioned getting struck by a taxi and receiving a sizable settlement, but Nick knew no such thing had ever happened. Perhaps Aunt Betty hadn't wanted to admit to a stranger that her own mother had hidden her fortune from her own child? Nick could understand that—he cherished memories of his mother and his father, and he rarely talked about the former's tendency to drink too much and the latter's proclivity for harsh corporal punishment when Nick stepped out of line.

Or was it that Aunt Betty had crafted her original letter to her fellow assassin in such a way as to create maximum sympathy for herself and her cause? Nick certainly couldn't rule out that possibility, especially in light of his aunt's newfound craftiness in other areas. He remembered her recent e-mail advising him to tell people what they wanted to hear as a way of motivating them to give you what you want. Perhaps Aunt Betty had chosen to tell her story in a way that would motivate Freddy's assassin to carry out his unpleasant task. And, as Leo Lentricchia's letter showed, he'd certainly been motivated by sympathy for the poor old lady whose peace and quiet were being ruined by a lowlife.

Interesting thought...that Aunt Betty and Joe Castro had been equally skilled in the art of manipulation. But no matter. Nick's mind was made up. "Solving" the crimes to get the promotion he wanted, telling the world about Joe's double life, contacting Joe's agent and offering to write the book for him—none of that would happen. He couldn't expose Joe's secret, couldn't break the code of silence that binds all cops. Someday he might need to take advantage of that code himself. Besides, once he exposed the truth, all his power to "make justice happen" would disappear. That power was too great a gift to exchange for a promotion or a book deal.

* * *

He took an afternoon to shred every document and photo in the filing cabinet. The one document he kept was Joe's letter to him, the one tucked into the folder at the rear of Drawer A. Then he took the bags of shredded paper to the recycling center, threw them out of his truck, and returned to his apartment.

Sitting at his kitchen table, he looked at the calendar hanging on the wall. It was a little more than a month after his visit to Leo's worksite in the Bronx. He picked up his cell phone, blocked his phone number, and punched in a sequence of numbers he'd memorized.

A woman's voice said, "Hello?"

"Hi, Mrs. Lentricchia? This is Mario, Leo's friend from high school. Hope you remember me? I moved to California but I'm back for a little while, and I'm getting in touch with some old friends. Is Leo around?"

Mrs. Lentricchia inhaled quickly. "No, I'm sorry, Mario, he's not here."

"Can you give him a message that I called? Or can you tell me how to find him?"

"I'm sorry, I don't know where he is." Her voice cracked. "He moved out a few weeks ago. Good-bye."

Lillian Smith

Dear Lenore:

Hey girl. You'll never guess where I am. Me & the kids are on a Greyhound Bus headed to the East Coast. They are asleep in the seats next to me and I am writing this letter.

Yes you heard me right. I am escaping for good, I hope. I can't believe it, it all happened so fast. I tried calling you before I left but your cell phone was disconnected. Did he get your number again? That's why I buy those throwaway phones where you use up the minutes and then get a new number. You should do the same, you think you can outsmart him but girl he is smarter than you. I hate to say it but you have admitted it yourself so you should take precautions like I do.

So let me start from the beginning. And that means I have to tell you something I never told you before. I know you'll forgive me because I was just following advice Marilyn gave me. I think I might have mentioned her once or twice, she was a counselor I had at a shelter in Tennessee, before I moved to Oklahoma and then Colorado, which is where I was before we met in Fresno. She said Jeff kept tracking me down because I wasn't covering my tracks good enough, I had to think of myself as being in something like the witness protection program. But the government wasn't going to help me like they do for people who rat out the Mafia so I had to do it myself, she said. Marilyn said I should have a simple easy name, one that would make us blend in even better, and that I shouldn't tell anyone my real name, not even new friends I made. So as soon as me & the kids got to Oklahoma I changed not only my name but also the kids' names. The problem was I used my real first name and the name of the street (LaFarge) I used to live on with Jeff, which was stupid I guess. He put two and two together and that's how he found us. So for the next name change I needed something even more basic, and that's how I became Lillian Smith. I got the first name from a Lillian Vernon catalog that was on the front seat of the car as I was driving to the Mercy House in Boulder, and the Smith part should explain itself.

Before I knew you my name was Claudia d'Arget. I lied when I said I grew up in Florida. I am actually from a town in New Jersey called Bloomfield. It is not far from New York City. My life in Bloomfield sucked from the minute I was born until the minute I left. My father was a shit who abandoned us when I was a kid, and then I had to deal with living with my mother. She was a bitter hateful old hag. She never stopped feeling sorry for herself after my father left and she took it out on all of us. I'm not an only child like I told you, I actually had two brothers and my mother took turns deciding which one of us she hated the most. Most of the time I was the main target because my father never really believed I was his daughter, though how could that be, everyone said how much I looked like him. She said I was the one who made him leave, and I believed it for years. For so long it never occurred to me she was lying, she probably made the whole story up as an excuse to take her frustrations out on me.

She also hated men (and now I understand why) so she had issues with my brothers too. My older brother Zack was a good guy, good at sports and girls liked him but he needed discipline and he started acting up when my father left and she couldn't handle it. He always thought he was tough so he joined the Navy. We kept in touch for a little while, he sent me postcards every so often. Then he started a fight in a bar somewhere in Asia and got stabbed and that was the end of him. I found out about it when one of his navy buddies found his address book and called everyone to tell them. I was with Jeff at the time and he answered the phone when the guy called. He didn't tell me my brother was dead until a month after Zack was buried. He didn't want me asking him for the money to go to Zack's funeral.

It was a really tough time for me and I cried for weeks. I mean, I had my own troubles to worry about but I loved my brother, and if my father hadn't left we could have grown up normal and been close and there for each other. But our lives were just so fucked up and we had to fend for ourselves and that meant we never saw each other. Poor Zack didn't deserve what he got, him and my father were actually pretty close and I can only imagine the pain he didn't show when my father left and never called any of us again. The worst part is, I bet my mother hung up the phone when Zack's navy buddy called to tell her. And everything sort of hit me, all that self-pity (remember Taryn's group sessions when she used to say there was nothing worse? she was so right about that) and it just sort of tore me apart. And that drove Jeff crazy, he said he couldn't stand the crying and each time I cried he was going to cut me up with a piece of the old mirror from the basement, and even though I tried to hide my tears he could see them from a mile away, and he'd go to the cellar and come up with one of those shards—which is why my back looks the way it does, and now you know the real reason why, and it's not because I got burned on a BBQ grate when I was a kid.

And then there was my younger brother Freddy. He didn't have a lot of ambition and that drove my mother crazy, she said he was going to grow up to be as useless as his (my) father was. So she drove him insane too until finally him & his girlfriend packed up and moved to L.A. That was years ago and it was the last I heard of him. Not that he even told me himself. I heard about in a postcard from Zack when he said something like,

"Ma is in the house by herself now, Freddy moved to California." I guess I could have tried to get more details but by that point I had already moved twice to get away from Jeff and that took all my energy, protecting the kids and also myself. And what was Freddy going to do to help me, anyway? He was always into drugs, I know he dealt them when we were teenagers, and there was no way I was going to let the kids be around anything like that. Besides I wouldn't have wanted to put my brother in danger, especially after what Jeff did to my landlord in Tennessee who was only trying to help me. And I still have nightmares about that because he had young kids and now those kids have no father, just like I had no father and my kids have no father.

I actually did think for about 10 seconds about trying to call my mother after Jeff found me in Oklahoma. I was in a panic because Jeff had set my neighbor's trailer on fire and destroyed his car, all because he saw the guy talking to me. As soon as I heard what happened, I knew Jeff was there, but of course the police didn't believe me. And when I came home from work with the kids and saw his motorcycle parked in front of my trailer I knew if I went in I would not come out alive. So I just turned around and kept driving, and I pulled off the road and actually thought about calling my mother for the first time in ten years. Jeff had no idea I was from New Jersey, he would never think to look for me there, and she had a whole house and she never met her grandkids. But who was I kidding, I knew she'd hang up on me the second she heard my voice because I was nothing but a slut and a whore and she didn't need the neighbors knowing what she'd raised. Besides, helping out her daughter and grandkids would have forced her to do some explaining to everyone. Before he died Zack told me he heard a rumor that my mother was telling people I was dead, just to get rid of me permanently I guess. Bottom line, there was no hope she'd help me, plus I didn't want help from her anyway. So I went to the hospital because the police never help and I had nowhere else to go, and I talked to some lady who told me about the Mercy House in Boulder, and I drove for sixteen hours until I got there. When I got there I told them my name was Lillian Smith and that's what everyone called me. The counselors tried to get my real name out of me but I said if they made me tell them, I would leave. But they saw how desperate and scared I was, which is why they got me and the kids out of there and into the Fresno Mercy House in a few days.

I hated leaving Fresno, I really did. We liked it there. I hated it when you moved to Eureka but I think we both knew it had to happen, we have to go where it makes sense for us to go, where we can have help. Somehow I thought we could stay in Fresno forever, I mean there was no way Jeff could find me there, right? But a couple of weeks ago I started getting crank calls at night, someone hanging up as soon as they heard my voice. Once or twice I thought I saw someone in the shadows near the apartment. I am not paranoid but you can't go through what me & you have gone through, and not have a feeling when something is wrong. One night a girl who worked at the diner with me drove me home because my car was broken down again, and the next day her windshield was smashed and all her tires were slashed. She had no idea what happened but I knew immediately, and I just wanted to scream and cry in frustration that we had to MOVE AGAIN, so I called Billie Jo at Mercy House and she was fabulous as always, me & the kids went there and they started looking for a new place for us.

Meanwhile, and this is what you won't believe, they were going to my apartment every day to pick up my mail for me, get things we needed, etc. After we were at the shelter for a week, they brought me a big envelope that looked all official. I opened it and I couldn't believe my eyes. It turned out my mother died more than a year ago. She did such a good job of telling everyone I was dead that nobody thought I was alive, so nobody looked for me to tell me. But they did find my brother Freddy, living in California still. And he ended up with my mother's house in NJ because she left it to him in her will. He had a free house so why wouldn't he move into it? Which is what he did, and that's where he was living for the last year.

But, and this is the terrible part, Freddy was murdered a few months ago. Nobody knows who did it but it seems like he was selling drugs out of the house and a deal went bad. So in that packet I get news that my two remaining family members are dead. Who cares about my mother, but I cried anyway for everything we could have had, and I cried harder for Freddy and for Zack too, and for myself and being deprived of a reasonable decent family that could have stuck together and helped each other out, like families are supposed to do.

Freddy died without a will, and there was no one to get the house, so the government had to figure out what to do with it. They started researching everything and talking to some neighbors of my mother's, and they talked to a girlfriend I had when I was about 10 years old who said "I heard Claudia died, but I never really believed it." And she told the guy about how my mother sent me away to Maryland when I was 15 because I was pregnant, and he did some poking around, and that is how they traced me, no matter how hard you try to cover your tracks they always find you.

And so it turns out the house in Bloomfield, NJ, that awful house where I grew up, is mine now. Free and clear. Even though I don't believe in God, I might start because I feel like he did this for me. I sold the car and bought the bus tickets, and now we are on our way to NJ. With the checks I get from the government I should be able to keep the house and have a decent place for the kids to grow up. Bloomfield was always boring but it's friendly and the kids will like it, and even though I hate that house it is still *a house of my own*.

What worries me is that if the government can find me after all these years of being "dead," then Jeff can too. I won't be free from him until he's dead or I am. I feel sort of guilty thinking that all those innocent people who live on ■■■■ ■■■■■■■ Road might have to deal with Jeff at some point, but I have to take care of myself and my kids, and for now this is the best (& only) way to do it.

OK this bus is stopping finally, some place in some state I don't really care about. It's still a long way to NJ but finally, finally I might have a life again. I'm going to try not to think about Jeff, but of course I'm going to keep my eyes and ears open and watch the kids like a hawk.

I'll write more when I get settled, after I get a new phone number. Wish me luck girl. I hope you haven't moved & this letter reaches you.

Love,
Lillian

A

Joe Castro

Nick—

The files speak for themselves. Everything you need to know is in here. I shredded the letters from the people who didn't make it into the final circle. They're irrelevant.

Are you shocked? Probably not.

You're asking why, right?

Because something had to be done about Garanowicz. I'd always known it, but when you coach kids you understand even more how vulnerable they are.

Because people are so fucking stupid. They eat and drink and shop and shit, and they have no idea someone could be plotting their death. A book like mine would have shaken them out of their complacency, shown them what the world is really like.

Because I wanted to know the mind of a murderer. They'll never tell us, and their lawyers won't let them. But I have a theory, and I wanted to test it. It's not about money or passion—it's about power and control, or the lack of it. And I was right. I never worried that any of them wouldn't do what they signed up to do—they were all powerless, and they all wanted to kill someone. I just made sure that each one got the assignment that was best for them. The dean didn't bother me so much, which is why I gave him to the priest.

But most of all, because I could. Because I wanted to.

And why not save myself? Why should I, Nick? The job finally broke me down. I fought it. I thought coaching would show me some goodness in the world. It did, but not enough. Every night when I put my gun down I thought about sticking it down my throat and pulling the trigger. Father Tomás was helping. Just by talking with me. Never judging me, just trying to help me see the good.

To find out the man I trusted more than anyone else (yes, more than I trusted you, Nick) could do this to me—there had to be a reason for it. The man who counseled me and promised he'd keep my secret decided to use my secret against me. He was stupid, too—he believed me when I told him about the supposed double blind system, not realizing I'd open his letter and discover that he believed I deserved to die. Yes, this man of God, this wise and kind man, conferred with God and decided my life has no merit.

And he was right, Nick. God himself decreed I should not be allowed to live. And when your God makes that decision, you can't fight it. So I decided not to.

I'll be interested to see how the English professor kills me. She's been nosing around the club lately. I suspect she'll invite herself here. I'm thinking it will probably be poison. She's tiny. I could flatten her with one finger. But I'm not going to. You'll know how she did it when you watch the tapes.

You decide what you're going to do now. But I have a recommendation. Justice is much simpler than anyone allows it to be. So make it happen, however you see fit.

Joe

Acknowledgments

I owe a debt of gratitude to Lorraine Patsco, who read the manuscript in early drafts and offered many superb suggestions. I would also like to thank my wonderful editor, Christian Alighieri, as well as Senior Editor Emily Marlowe, for their support, their kindness, and their friendship.

This special two-in-one edition also includes the sequel, *Good Boys Never Win*.

"Rigolosi, a completely fresh voice in the mystery genre, writes with gusto...Don't miss this book." —*Library Journal*

"Very clever and unique...Rigolosi keep[s] his readers on edge with his easy-to-read narrative, lovable characters, and intriguing plot." —Bookpleasures.com

FICTION/SUSPENSE
978-0-9773787-3-9/ 0-9773787-3-X

Read the first chapter of *Who Gets the Apartment?* online at
www.whogetstheapartment.com

COMING IN 2008

Androgynous Murder House Party

Tales from the Back Page #3

Six friends gather for a holiday weekend at the Long Island estate of independently wealthy snob Robin Anders. As near-deadly accidents and mishaps mount, Robin is faced with the possibility that one of the six may be plotting murder most foul. But a larger question looms in the air: Are Robin, Lee, Alex, Chris, Law, and J men or women?

FICTION/SUSPENSE
978-0-9773787-6-0 / 0-9773787-6-4

Ransom
note Press

About the Author

Steven Rigolosi is the director of market research and development at a Manhattan-based publisher of scientific books. *Circle of Assassins* is his second novel. After years of living in Manhattan, he now lives in Northern New Jersey, where he is at work on future installments of the *Tales from the Back Page* series. His e-mail address is <u>srigolosi@yahoo.com</u>.